Scattered
A Post Apocalyptic Survival Thriller
Kevin Partner

Scribbleit

Copyright © 2024 by Kevin Partner

All rights reserved.

No portion of this book may be reproduced in any form without written permission from the publisher or author, except as permitted by U.K. copyright law.

Contents

1. Chapter 1 — 1
2. Chapter 2 — 13
3. Chapter 3 — 23
4. Chapter 4 — 33
5. Chapter 5 — 44
6. Chapter 6 — 54
7. Chapter 7 — 64
8. Chapter 8 — 76
9. Chapter 9 — 88
10. Chapter 10 — 99
11. Chapter 11 — 110
12. Chapter 12 — 122
13. Chapter 13 — 134
14. Chapter 14 — 144
15. Chapter 15 — 157

16. Chapter 16	168
17. Chapter 17	179
18. Chapter 18	191
19. Chapter 19	205
20. Epilogue	215
Read The Stranger	219
Read The Stranger	220
About Kev	221

Chapter 1

It was too cold to enjoy fishing, but they had to eat, so Solly Masters cast his line again and pulled the blanket around him. Ross, Jaxon and two other boys were sitting by the bank with fishing poles they'd found on an expedition into Hagerstown. None of them had ever fished before and their attempts to assemble their rods, thread line, tie on hooks and impale bits of earthworm would have been comical if the situation hadn't been so deadly serious.

Until now, they'd been relying entirely on scavenged supplies, but their safety depended on remaining unnoticed. Every time they went into town they risked being attacked by desperate individuals and the more organized groups that were now springing up. So, they had to become as self-sufficient as possible as quickly as they could, though Conococheague Creek was not proving generous so far.

Solly glanced at the boys along the bank. Ross sat next to him, hunched over the rod that sat across his legs and gazing out at the river where his float bobbed on the sullen surface. Since they'd discovered the farmhouse that was now serving as their base of operations, Ross had transformed from a taciturn teenager to an open, kind and generous young man. Most surprisingly, he and Jaxon had become firm friends and the two of them were chatting from time to time as they sat on the bank.

The transformation of Ross was one small miracle in a world gone dark. Five weeks ago, Solly had been an unemployed and newly divorced app developer from Texas living in a rented apartment in downtown Manhattan.

"What's so funny?" Ross said.

"Funny? Nothing. Call it gallows humor," Solly responded, realizing he'd chuckled out loud. "I was just remembering how I'd thought my world had ended when I lost my job. And then it actually did end, and I realize just how insignificant my problems were back then. Nothing I couldn't fix. And now..." He shrugged.

Ross tightened his line and then blew on his hands to warm them. "You're pretty awesome, Sol, but I don't think you can fix the entire world."

Jaxon called from the other side of Ross. "How do you eat an elephant, Solly?"

"One bite at a time," Solly and Ross chimed in response.

"Well this farmhouse, it's our first bite," Jaxon said.

Solly smiled and transferred his gaze out to the creek where his float bobbed. *One bite at a time* had been their mantra as soon as they'd chosen the farmhouse as their new base of operations. There was so much to do to make it habitable and secure, then to bring the children and babies—not to mention Arnold who'd long ago lost his legs to diabetes—let alone find a way to care for and feed them. So Solly had explained the principle of breaking a task down into manageable chunks and only worrying about the next one. The unintended consequence being that it was quoted back to him at every opportunity.

"My eyes are going funny," Ross said. "When I look away from the river, it seems as though the bank's moving."

With a blur of movement, Jaxon raised his arm. A fish leaped out of the water before plunging back beneath the surface. "I got one!"

"Gently does it!" Solly called. "Don't break the line. Just reel it in slow." He watched as Jaxon guided the fish into the bank, then handed his rod to Ross before bending down.

"Yuck, it's slimy!" he called out, recoiling.

Solly went to join him. "It's not slimy, it's cold and wet," he said, feeling the thing wriggling in his hands. He had no idea what species it was, but it was a good size, a foot or so in length, and looked edible.

"Nice one, Jaxon. Now, a few more of these and we can have fried fish tonight."

His mouth watered at the prospect, and he was just picturing it in his mind's eye when a cry went up from the direction of the farmhouse.

"Uncle Solly!"

He turned to see a girl standing on the bank above him, puffing. "What is it, Kayla?"

"There's a man!"

He leaped up and drew the gun from his pocket. "Where?"

"At the farm. Landon's got him covered, but Auntie Janice told me to come fetch you."

Ross and Jaxon stood up, but Solly waved them back down again. "You stay here but keep your ears open."

He climbed the bank and headed off at a trot toward the farmhouse, fear coursing through his veins. They'd been discovered.

THE MAN STOOD WITH his hands held high at the foot of the steps leading up to the farmhouse. Landon sat in a rocking chair, his shotgun aimed directly at the man's head with Janice beside him. As soon as she caught sight of Solly, she waved, and the visitor turned to face him.

He wore a long brown leather coat with a matching wide brimmed hat that cast a shadow over his eyes. He was white, lean and unshaven, but he didn't look desperate. And he wasn't frightened.

"My name is Jeremiah," he said in a cut glass English accent as Solly approached. "I have come to collect the package Khaled entrusted to you. Is it still here?"

"What does he mean?" Landon called. The young man had largely recovered from a bullet wound to the leg but still wasn't fully mobile. He was spending his convalescence in a rocking chair on the porch wrapped in a blanket made of crochet squares of seemingly random colors.

Solly didn't answer either Jeremiah or Landon. He approached the stranger and searched him for weapons, emerging with a snub-nosed revolver and hunting knife that he handed to Janice.

"Follow me," he said before leading Jeremiah up the stairs and in through the door.

Arnold wheeled himself out of the living room, but the question died on his lips as Solly shook his head before crossing the hall and opening the door to the room that had become his. He gestured the man into his desk chair and stood over him, revolver in hand.

Throughout, the man had remained calm and relaxed, as if everything was happening exactly as expected.

Solly opened with the most important question. "How did you find me?"

The man's face spread in a self-satisfied smile. "So, you *are* the man Khaled gave it to? Excellent."

"Answer my question," Solly said. "How did you know I was here?"

Jeremiah shrugged. "I didn't," he began. Then, holding his hands up to quell Solly's fury, he said, "Look, I will answer, but I am hungry and thirsty. Could we not discuss this like civilized men over a pot of coffee and a bite to eat?"

"I don't feel inclined to be 'civilized' when I don't know whether the safety of the people here is under threat."

"Then I can reassure you that your secret is safe with me. You are in no more danger now than you were before I located you. Now, do you have the means to make me a coffee or must I remain uncaffeinated?"

Solly took him through to the large kitchen of the farmhouse, ordered the children out and poured a mug of coffee from the pot warming on the stove.

"Ah, that's so good," Jeremiah said, sipping the rich black liquid with relish. "It's been a few days since I had a freshly made cup of joe."

Solly watched the man's face carefully as he drank. His joy was genuine, unless he was a masterful actor, and the lines around his eyes opened as he swallowed, revealing pale pink skin beneath a layer of dirt and grime that suggested some days on the open road.

"Now, tell me how you found me," Solly said.

Jeremiah put his cup down. "I didn't find you, I found the cylinder. It has a tracking device, though it is no longer transmitting. This was the last known location and, when I saw that you match the description Khaled gave me, I knew it must still be here."

"But if you found me, that means others can," Solly said, "which puts the children here in danger."

"No, the frequency is only known to a few people, none of whom are a threat to your safety. I must say, though, I was expecting to find you, the boy and the woman, not an entire community. A community made up largely, it seems, of children. There is an interesting story behind this, I perceive."

Solly shook his head. "No, you don't get to change the subject. What do you want of me?"

"I wish you to hand over the package that Khaled gave you."

"Assuming I still have it," Solly said in as noncommittal a voice as he could manage. "If you really do come from Khaled, you'll know the codeword he gave me before handing it over."

Jeremiah chuckled. "Yes, he is not the world's most sophisticated secret agent, is he? I believe the codeword he chose was *raven*. Inspired, no doubt, by the carrion birds gorging themselves on the former population of New York."

"It's no joking matter," Solly said, icily.

"I'm sorry. You are quite correct. Five weeks ago, a virus was unleashed on humankind that, in one night, killed more people than the bubonic plague managed in centuries."

Solly reached out and grabbed his arm. "It *was* a virus? How could it possibly get around the country so quickly?"

"Not a biological virus, to be sure, but just as deadly. And it didn't affect the US alone—this was a global killing. In one night, 90% of the world's people died and another 5% joined them over the following couple of days." He leaned back and pushed the mug away. "We have to seek solace in simple pleasures in the face of such devastation."

Rubbing his eyes, Solly slumped onto the table, allowing his revolver to rest inches from Jeremiah, who seemed to ignore it. Global? Solly hadn't given much thought to the rest of the world until the past week or so. He was still working on getting the farm's wind turbine working so they'd have at least some access to electricity and, hopefully, any news transmissions.

"So you mean a technological virus," Solly said, finally. "BonesWare?"

Jeremiah nodded solemnly. "Yes. Developed to save human lives, it turned into the carrier for the deadliest weapon ever created."

"But I've got Bones, and so have most of the older kids here. Why did we survive?"

"That is a difficult question to answer, but I will say this—it was unleashed by the Lee Corporation, and they intend to release another wave that will bring the survivors of the apocalypse under their control."

Solly felt all at sea. Half an hour ago, he'd been fishing in the local creek and now he was talking about the end of the world, mark two.

"What do you mean?"

Shrugging, Jeremiah said, "I don't know much more, but 98% of the US population had Bones devices, and the vast majority of those died immediately. That still leaves 10 million alive, plus another six million who hadn't been implanted. Imagine if the Lee Corporation could gain control over the remaining implants. They would hold an ax above the head of everyone with the device. That would be power indeed."

"So, tell me Jeremiah," Solly said, "how is it that you are so very well informed?"

Jeremiah sighed. "There is only so much I can reveal, I'm afraid. I ask you to take it on trust that I am working against the interests of the Lee Corporation and that your life and those of the people here will be all the safer once the package is removed."

"What is it exactly?"

"As I said, I cannot tell you everything because I do not know everything. I merely know that the package is of vital importance in preventing the second wave and I have been given a grid reference to deliver it to."

Solly got up from the table and, keeping his eye firmly on the visitor, poured them both another cup of coffee. "Where is it going?"

"I am under strict instructions to keep that confidential," Jeremiah said, again sensing Solly's temper flaring and holding up his hands. "Not because you are not to be trusted, but because the fewer who know, the less the risk of the Lees getting their hands on it. That really would be the end."

Solly sat down again opposite the man. "So, you're all that stands between the Lee Corporation and the second wave?"

Jeremiah let out a rich laugh that bounced around the kitchen. "It seems ridiculous, does it not? I see why you struggle to believe me—I do not look like much of a hero. Now, will you help me?"

"I haven't decided yet," Solly answered, noting how Jeremiah's face darkened. "You look and smell as though you've been on the road for a long time. Luckily for you, it's bath night tonight, so we'll be heating water. I suggest you enjoy our hospitality today and we'll make a decision tomorrow."

"You will allow me to roam freely?" Jeremiah said, his face clouded with suspicion.

Solly shook his head. "You can enjoy my company for the afternoon, we can go fishing."

IT WAS DARK. THE babies had been bathed and the children and adults had taken precisely timed showers. Solly had been rather proud of his somewhat Heath Robinson method of getting the hot water from the fire pit outside to the hot water tank in the attic, but he'd foregone his shower and had sent Jeremiah in instead.

He left Ross outside the door of the bathroom and ran downstairs to the basement, leaving the intervening doors open so Ross could warn him if there was any trouble. Using a candle to light his way, Solly went over to the thick oak table that had once, presumably, graced the kitchen but had then endured a second life as a workbench. On it sat a metal safe.

Luckily the safe had been open when he'd discovered it and the combination had been written on a paper label on the inside of the door. Designed to withstand the house falling on top of it, the safe seemed the best place to put the cylinder that Khaled had given him.

Solly's paranoid streak had not lessened since the end of the world, and he just wanted to check it was still there. It wasn't beyond the bounds of possibility, after all, that Jeremiah had a confederate who might have infiltrated the building while Solly was occupied.

He keyed in the combination and pulled the door open. Solly breathed a sigh of relief as he saw the silver cylinder lying there untouched. He examined it, looking for any indication of which part might be transmitting its location.

Suddenly, as he pulled it clear of the safe, he heard the electronic wail of an alarm coming from the upper floor.

Chapter 2

Bella

BELLA MASTERS STOOD ON the balcony and watched the waves rolling in. It was a gray winter's day, and a chilly breeze blew in off the ocean. A few months before, Crystal Beach had teemed with families enjoying the golden sands and now the only sound was the wind in the palm trees and the crying of the gulls.

She hadn't told anyone of her plans, not even Nathan, the injured soldier whose sacrifice had bought time for Bella, her father and her two children to escape. Solly's parents had owned this beach house for many years, and she had fond memories of days spent together enjoying the simple pleasures that now seemed lost forever.

Bella had been relieved to find the house empty when they'd arrived in their shot-up SUV. She'd stopped at the home of Solly's mother and left the children in the car as she went inside to find the old woman long dead in the living room. It had taken every ounce of self-control to stop herself from running back out again, so overwhelming was the stench and the sickeningly compelling sight of the remains of someone Bella had loved. Grief and guilt hit her like buckshot out of a double-barreled shotgun. She had thought of the old woman many times since the night of the Long Fall but had decided the trip was too far to risk. She was disgusted with herself, especially since she'd braved a similar distance to fetch her own father. But then, when she'd set off for his care home, she hadn't known that the world was falling apart around them. Bella almost felt that Solly's father, who'd died the previous year, had gotten off lightly.

She'd found the keys to the beach house in their usual place and had just been about to go when an idea struck her. If Solly was still alive and made it back to Texas, he would first go to their home and then he'd be sure to come here to check on his mother. So, she scribbled a short note and left it in plain view. Only he would understand what she'd written, and she allowed herself to picture him arriving at the house and walking up the steps. Solid dependable Solly.

The house was on Redfish Lane, a light blue wooden building raised on stilts against the occasional freak storm. It had taken many hours to get there, and Bella had been forced to pick her way around abandoned cars, trying desperately not to run over anything lying in the road. Al had taken over for part of the journey, but his eyes weren't what they had been, and Bella had decided it was safest to drive by moonlight, so they were reduced to crawling along as she squinted into the darkness.

She felt a sudden weight on her shoulders.

"Thanks, Pop," she said, settling down into one of a pair of chairs on the veranda and drawing the blanket around her. She reached up, took the glass and sipped gently. "Brandy?"

"Rum," Al said. "Jake says Silas found a box of bottles and gave him one."

Bella's mood darkened. Silas Roux was the de facto head of the community they'd found here when they'd arrived. They'd barely gotten out of the car after a long and exhausting journey when he'd turned up and welcomed them to the neighborhood. Since that night—three weeks ago now—more people had arrived to occupy other houses in Redfish Lane and the other beach front roads. They'd generally arrived in small groups that had formed through strangers meeting on the road and banding together for protection.

Silas had been a lifeguard and surfer and, whether by design or accident, the larger community had coalesced around him, attracted, it seemed, by his easy-going nature and "anything goes" attitude. He'd certainly had an impact on Maddie and Jake, who were spending an increasing amount of time with him.

"He's no *shmendrik*," Al remarked, reading her mind. "I don't see any evil in him, and I think we have to trust the kids to look out for themselves. After all, Jake isn't really a child any longer."

Jake's sixteenth birthday last week should have been a time of celebration, but he'd spent most of it with his newly found friends. Not that this birthday bore any resemblance to the last one. She'd argued with Solly over the phone about whether they should get their son the PS5 he'd asked for. Predictably, Solly had been on the boy's side and

Jake had been granted his wish. The console now sat in his old bedroom, as dead as the country. That was assuming the family house hadn't been consumed by the fire that Al had ignited in the motorbikes parked outside during their escape.

"He's become so much wilder since we got here," she said.

Al let out an amused grunt. "You mean he's gotten harder to control. Welcome to the rest of your life, *Tokhter.*"

The sun set behind gray clouds over the Gulf of Mexico as Bella and her father sat beside a guttering hurricane lamp and waited for the children to return.

"Mom!"

Bella was jerked out of a deep sleep, flailing around before grabbing her glasses from the little table by the bed and sitting up. "Maddie? What's happened?"

The girl stood beside the bed, a candle in her shaking hand.

"It's Jake, he's been hurt bad!"

Panic flooded Bella's mind, and she was fully awake in an instant. She swung her legs out of bed and stumbled around in the dark to find clothes. "What happened?"

"We were at a party over at the Sanchez's, and he got into a fight," Maddie said, her words tumbling out, "and he fell over the railing and onto the sand. He's not dead, but he's hurt, Mom."

Bella was now charging into Al's room. "Dad! Jake's been hurt, we have to go."

Maddie followed her downstairs.

"Has he broken anything?"

"I don't know, but, but..."

Bella stopped and grabbed her daughter's arms. "Spit it out, Maddie!"

"He landed on a deck chair, and it broke, and it stabbed him. I told them not to move him until you got there, but I don't know if they've listened to me. I came to find you as fast as I could."

Letting Maddie go, Bella pulled on her coat as her father hobbled down the stairs. "Fill your grandfather in, and follow me," she said as she flung the door open and ran into the night.

She found him lying in what remained of a wooden chair, draped in a blanket. Silas was kneeling beside him holding his hand, but he got up as he saw Bella approach and handed her a flashlight.

"Mrs. Masters, I'm really sorry. I don't know how it happened. Everything was cool and then... it wasn't."

"I'll deal with you later," she said. "Now make yourself useful for once and get me some bandages."

She got onto the floor, crying out as she felt a cold slickness on her knee. "Oh, my poor boy," she said. She shone the flashlight onto his legs and saw that while the right one moved freely, the left leg was pinned to the wreckage of the chair somehow. Looking more closely, she could see that a wooden slat had fractured in the fall and penetrated the back of his calf.

She heard footsteps approaching. "I can't find any bandages, Mrs. Masters."

"Call yourself a leader?"

"Actually, I don't," Silas responded quietly.

More steps and a green first aid box appeared over Bella's shoulder. "Here... thought you could... use this," Al panted. "*Oy vey*," he added on seeing Jake's leg. "You're going to have to get that out."

"You think?" Bella snapped. "Silas, is there a doctor in the community?"

"No ma'am, they don't stick around."

She turned back to Al. "We need to get him home, so we can clean it. Get some bandages out and when I lift his leg, help me wrap them around the wound."

"What if it's cut an artery?"

"I think there'd be a lot more blood if that had happened," she said, keeping the thought that Jake would also be dead by now in that case to herself. "Honey, this is going to hurt, but we've got to get it out before we can do anything else. Okay?"

Jake looked pale and sweat ran down his cheeks as he nodded. Al took one hand and Maddie the other as Bella clenched her jaw and felt beneath the boy's leg until she found where the wood fragment punctured the skin.

Gently, she exerted pressure on the back of Jake's thigh.

"Aaaah!!!" he cried, his legs writhing.

"Hold him still!" Bella called, "This has to come straight out, or it may break off inside him. Or tear something."

She wasn't listening as Al tried to soothe the boy while he and Maddie pressed down hard on his upper body. She focused entirely on bringing the leg upwards as, despite all they could do, it shook in Jake's agony. Suddenly it went still as Silas knelt beside her and wrapped his hands around Jake's ankle. "We'll get you something for the pain soon, Jake," he said. "Just hold on in there."

"It's coming!" Bella hissed as she raised the boy's leg inch by inch, trying desperately to ignore his cries of agony. "It's clear!"

Al handed her two rolls of bandage. He let go of Jake's arm and helped her wrap it around his leg, pants and all. Blood soaked the first roll almost immediately, so he took off his belt. "Wrap this around the top of his leg," he said. "And you, Silas, find us a needle and some dental floss—bring it to our place and if you're not there before us, there'll be hell to pay."

MADDIE RAN INTO THE party house and found two young men and a woman who'd been skulking in the shadows. Between them, they were able to lift Jake up and carry him the hundred yards to their beach house, get him up the steps and onto the kitchen table.

"And don't go far!" Al called as they exited. "We'll need help getting him into bed."

He wiped Jake's face, then looked at Bella. "You've done well *liebchen*, now let me take over from here.

I remember my army first aid training well enough. You comfort the boy."

"Maddie, boil up some water, quick as you can. We need to get this wound cleaned."

Silas appeared at the door to the kitchen. "Man, it was tough to find a needle, but I got it." He put it down. "I'll go help Maddie with the fire. I guess we ought to sterilize the needle."

"It's not his fault," Jake murmured. "He wasn't there when the fight started."

"What happened, son?" Bella asked as she gripped his hand.

Jake turned his pale face to her. "Sayed said something about Maddie. I don't reckon he knew she's my sister. I told him to apologize, and he swung at me."

"Good boy," Al said. He'd found a pair of scissors and was cutting the leg of Jake's pants away from beneath the improvised tourniquet. Jake winced as the old man then cut off the bandage and examined the wound. Blood oozed out. "Looks pretty clean. Ah, good timing, thanks."

Maddie placed a bowl of steaming water on the table. "I got it from the Walters' house—it's been boiled."

"Well done. Could you get me another bowl for the final clean up? And get that idiot Silas to make him a sweet tea," Al said. "Proper tea, mind, not that new age rubbish you lot drink these days."

Al took wadding from the first aid box and dipped it in the hot water; then, working by candlelight, he gently dabbed it into the wound. The wadding turned red, and the boy moaned as Al worked, but after a few minutes he declared himself satisfied. "I can't be certain there's nothing left inside, but we've got to just hope for the best. Now for the worst part. This is going to hurt, son."

Maddie returned with the tea and Jake took several sips before he allowed himself to be rolled onto his front. The next ten minutes were utter torture for him and for Bella.

The needle Silas had found was larger than Al would have like and with every stitch, Jake cried out and his limbs shook. In the end, they'd called for reinforcements so that each part of him was held down by one person and so the process sped up until, finally, it was over.

"Not exactly a neat job," Al said. "But it'll hold together, I think."

They rolled Jake over and Silas handed something to him. "Here, this'll help."

"What are you giving him?" Al roared, snatching the packet from Silas's hand. "Oh. Sorry."

"It's just a Hershey bar. If it's good enough for fending off Dementors, it should be cool for leg wounds," Silas said with a smile.

"Fending off what?" Al responded.

Bella put her arms around him. "It's okay, Dad. You've done brilliantly. Now, let's get him to bed."

A few minutes later, Jake was asleep, and the house had emptied of beach bums. "Well, he's not going to bleed to death, but I've told Silas to find some antibiotics," Bella said. "Are you going back to bed?"

The old man shook his head. "No, I'm wide awake after all that. I'm going to have another go at the controller."

He took a candle and went downstairs into the room that had been built in between the stilts holding up the house. Solly's father had installed a wind turbine a few years before, partly to provide backup during the power cuts that hit this exposed coastline occasionally, and partly for the challenge. Al shook his head as he settled down at the workbench. *Like father, like son.* Although he didn't generally admit it, he had become fond of Solly over the years, though he'd been puzzled by his decision to move across the country for a job fiddling with computers when he could have done the same thing in Houston.

Solly's father hadn't finished the installation before inconveniently dying a year or so ago. Al had discovered the half-built rats' nest of wires, plastic and metal when he'd first come down here and had made it his mission to get it working. But there had always been other things to do, and he wasn't a geek himself. If he got it working, then it'd charge up the bank of batteries that sat on a raised platform near the roof and they'd be able to run the radio and, perhaps, the TV from the inverter. There might be nothing to hear or see, but maybe the government was reestablishing itself and they were deaf to the announcements.

Al sat at the bench and raised the instruction manual for the charge controller to the candle. One last step and he could get the system working. One last step to reconnect them with the world outside.

Chapter 3

Solly

Solly watched as Jeremiah walked out of the farmhouse and then west along the creek road. He felt the burden of responsibility lift from his shoulders, and yet he was also nervous. Jeremiah had told him less than he knew about the events of five weeks ago, that much was obvious, and yet Solly was convinced that the little cylinder he'd handed over was indeed critical to preventing some future disaster. So, he followed Jeremiah.

Solly was now familiar enough with the lay of the land to be able to shadow Jeremiah without being seen. The creek ran on one side of the lane and on the other, the farm side, lay a sloped meadow of soggy grass and mud lined with trees and it was this cover that Solly used to watch Jeremiah as he walked along. He was heading for the Eisenhower highway where he would find a car and begin his journey to... wherever.

They'd talked for hours after the removal of the cylinder from the safe had triggered Jeremiah's alarm, but Solly hadn't learned much more about why it was so important, only that it *was*.

In the end, Solly had been forced to make a decision with limited information since Jeremiah could, or would, tell him no more. There was an endgame here that Solly couldn't see, and he suspected that even Jeremiah lacked some critical pieces of the jigsaw puzzle. It had been the safety of the children that had been the deciding factor, ultimately. The cylinder had a tracking device and, though it could be shielded in the safe, that didn't alter the fact that its last known location was the farmhouse. If Jeremiah could find them, then so could others. Though he insisted that the Lee Corporation didn't know the cylinder was missing, let alone how to find it, Solly wasn't so confident. It was hard to imagine that an organization with the power, it appeared, to kill 95% of the world's population could be outwitted by a few individuals with good intentions.

Solly peered from behind the trunk of a tree, taking care to direct his breath into the ground so that the mist didn't reveal his location should Jeremiah look this way. The man had his head down and was going at a great pace—hurrying to reach the highway, it seemed. Solly crouched down and ran across the field, his boots squelching in the boggy soil. Reaching the next stand of trees, he paused for a moment to catch his breath. Ironically all the exercise of the past weeks had left Solly fitter than he'd ever been, but he was no superman, and he could barely keep up with the dark figure striding along the lane.

He crossed a track that ran at right angles to the river and hid behind the wall of a neighboring farm. They'd checked it out soon after moving in to the farmhouse, and Solly was careful to avoid the barn where the rotting remains of the dairy herd lay.

He was just jogging along, wondering how long he would continue to follow Jeremiah, when he heard the sound of a car revving followed by the *pop pop* of small arms. Solly accelerated, keeping to the questionable cover of the trees that ran along the side of the road until he reached a bend and peered around it.

There, where the road widened as it joined the highway, a station wagon was parked with both doors open. Solly could see someone sheltering behind the nearer door, firing across the road. He caught sight of another figure, dressed in black military fatigues, moving away from the vehicle in a wide arc and guessed that while his colleague kept Jeremiah pinned down, he would attempt to outflank him.

Solly pulled the Ruger semiautomatic from his pocket and flipped the safety. Keeping himself as low as possible, he crossed the road and closed in on the figure sheltering behind the door. He could see past the car to a low brick wall that Jeremiah was hiding behind. The attacker was wearing armor, so it would take a decent shot to fell him and Solly took aim. Then, after a moment, he sighed and called out, "Put your weapon down!"

The figure spun around and was bringing his carbine to bear when a red mist exploded from his head, and he fell to the ground. Solly saw Jeremiah crouch back behind his cover and then, in a blur of movement, the second soldier appeared and fired at Jeremiah at point blank range. Solly sprinted toward the car and, as the soldier turned toward him, fired three times. The soldier fell to the ground and, after a moment's pause, Solly ran across the road and pointed his handgun down at the fallen man. One of the shots had punched through his jaw and smashed half his face. Solly put his hand over his mouth to hold back the bile rising in his throat, then turned to Jeremiah.

He'd taken a bullet to the side of the head and lay looking up at the sky. Solly looked again at the soldier he'd killed and saw the Lee Corporation logo on the man's chest. So, they did know about the cylinder, and they could track it, though their resources must be stretched if they'd sent a two-man squad to retrieve such an important device.

Solly went to move Jeremiah's head to a more natural angle but, as he did so, Jeremiah took a breath, looked him in the eye and whispered, "Take it to Arbroath..." Then he was truly gone, and Solly closed his eyes.

He hoped he'd never get used to being in the presence of death, but he also had to be practical, so he pulled Jeremiah's satchel from his shoulder and put it to one side then checked that the cylinder was inside. There was nothing in his pockets, so Solly covered Jeremiah's face with his hat, picked up his handgun and then knelt beside the nearest Lee Corporation soldier.

Keeping his gaze away from the ruined face, Solly took the carbine and two spare magazines, along with an ID card that was hanging on a chain around the soldier's neck.

The other attacker was lying face down behind the open door of the car in a pool of blood. Solly gasped as he rolled the body over and looked down into the face of a woman. She had short brown hair tucked into her combat helmet and no sign of an exit wound on her face. He choked back the tears as he looked at her. What kind of twisted reality allowed this?

He ripped the ID card from the chain around her neck. *Ellis Summers* followed by a series of numbers. The picture showed a serious looking young woman wearing a kepi. Just another victim of whatever her employers had unleashed on the world.

Solly took her carbine and spare magazines and piled them with those of the other soldier under a tree at the side of the road. He would come back later with a burial party and retrieve them.

HE'D PUT THE CYLINDER back into the safe in the basement and was sitting at the kitchen table with Janice and Arnold. Ross and Jaxon were currently driving the car used by the Lee Corporation soldiers onto the highway. There was a fair chance they would come looking for it and the scene of the ambush was too close to the farmhouse for comfort. Solly had given the boys strict instructions to only take the car a few miles and not to risk getting lost on their long walk back, but he was fretting about them as darkness fell outside.

Arnold was cradling a warm mug of coffee in his hands, "Arbroath, you say? Are you sure?"

"That's what I heard," Solly replied as he chewed on a slice of jerky, "but he was dying, there's no telling whether he knew what he was even saying."

"Sounds Scottish," Janice said.

"I don't imagine he was taking it across the Atlantic," Solly said. "If it's a place, it'll be here in the US."

He pulled a tattered road atlas out of Jeremiah's satchel and opened it. "This only covers the northeastern states," he said, "but Arbroath isn't in the index."

"If only we still had the internet," Janice said.

Solly smiled and reached out to take her hand. "At least we have bread. Smells delicious."

"You'll have to wait till the morning for that batch," Janice replied, returning his smile, "but I've got some of today's leftovers if you like."

Solly had eaten on his return to the farmhouse, but the prospect of an extra crust made his mouth water. Janice had made it her mission to work out how to bake bread reliably and, in the second week after they'd arrived at the farmhouse, had finally nailed it. They'd had no problem finding dried yeast in Hagerstown—it seemed the other looters hadn't seen its value. Flour had been a little harder to obtain until they'd found a barn full of processed sacks in a neighboring farm.

The farmhouse also had a small dairy herd that was allowed to roam in the meadows on either side. Learning how to milk them had been another of Janice's projects and they now had the means of nourishing the children and producing edible butter. Solly spread some of the light yellow paste onto his thick slice of crust and savored the taste. If there was one thing he'd learned in the past weeks, it was to take pleasure in the small things.

Janice watched him eat and squeezed his hand. Solly felt that familiar mixture of warmth and guilt as he looked back at her. They had a deep emotional connection that had matured into a gently physical one. Janice wasn't ready for their relationship to become intimate and, truth to tell, neither was Solly, but if he had to put a label on his feelings, he'd struggle to find a better word than *love*.

As for the little community they led, all it lacked now was power. He was no electrical engineer and had, so far, failed to get the wind turbine working properly. So, for now they relied on scavenging fuel for the generator in the basement which involved dangerous trips into the surrounding urban areas. This meant that the generator was run to a strict schedule, largely to power interior lights after dark.

They'd built so much in the past weeks, and yet it was so vulnerable. They now knew that the Lee Corporation could track the cylinder and, while the transmitter could be blocked by shielding, its last known location was near to the farmhouse. The only way to make the children safe was to take it elsewhere, knowing that, in doing so, Lee Corp would be able to follow him.

First things first, however—he needed to know where it had to go.

The next day, Solly stood outside the Washington County Library. It was a red brick building in the center of Hagerstown that, aside from some broken windows, had escaped relatively unharmed. It seemed that reading was undervalued in this postapocalyptic world.

Solly, Ross and Jaxon had set off at first light to walk the several miles into town. The boys were armed with hunting knives and Solly had his Ruger for company, but they saw no one until they were well inside the urban area when they noticed faces peering out from behind apartment windows, drapes twitching as they passed. It was a cold December day but in place of the colorful lights and decorations of previous years, there was nothing but trash and abandoned cars.

Solly stepped through the smashed glass of the library front door and peered into the gloom beyond, looking for any lurking trouble.

"We need the geography section," he said as Ross followed him inside.

"I have been in a library before," Ross said, "I know how they work."

A shape moved in the shadows and Solly spun around, gun in hand. "You are looking for a book? An atlas, maybe?"

It was the voice of an old woman, and Solly hid the Ruger as she shuffled forward.

"Who are you?" Ross said, unable to hide the disgust in his voice.

She was dressed in clothes that might once have been colorful, but she looked as though she hadn't changed them in weeks, perhaps since the night of the Long Fall itself. She looked deathly thin and peered out at them from behind teardrop shaped spectacles. "Do you have food, by any chance?" she said in a trembling and desperate voice.

Solly swung his pack from his shoulder and handed over a couple of energy bars. She swooped on them like a starving dog, barely giving herself time to open the wrappers before chewing on them. Solly pressed his water bottle into her hand as she began to choke. When she'd finished the bars, she straightened herself up and shook her head sadly. "I am sorry, I know I'm a mess. But Doris never came in, so I couldn't go home. The library must be manned, you see, or they'll take away our funding."

"You've been here for five weeks?"

She shrugged. "Has it been that long? I guess so. The food in the staff break room ran out a long time ago, but the water still works and there's always the rain. Now, are you looking for a book?"

Solly decided his only option was to play along. "Yes, we're trying to find out if there's a place called Arbroath."

"There's certainly a town called Arbroath in Scotland," she said. "'It is in truth not for glory, nor riches, nor honors, that we are fighting, but for freedom—for that alone, which no honest man gives up but with life itself.' The Declaration of Arbroath. Some say it was the seed that led to the Declaration of Independence centuries later."

"Is there a place of the same name in the US?"

"What? Oh. No, not that I've heard of. But then, I don't know every town and city in the United States. Not quite. "

The old woman shuffled off into the gloom, followed by Solly and the boys. It grew darker and darker as they approached the center of the library, far from the windows, and Solly almost bumped into her as she emerged, book in hand. "If it's in the US, we'll find it in here."

She put the atlas down on a table beneath one of the outer windows and turned to the index at the back. The book was a couple of feet tall and Solly breathed in the smell of printed paper and decaying librarian as she turned the pages. She found the beginning of the index and Solly watched as she ran her finger down the page.

"Aha! I've found it!" she said, delighted. She immediately closed the book and then flicked through the pages until she found the one she was looking for.

"C3," she muttered and Solly watched as her finger navigated the continental United States. Left, left, up and up it went. "There it is."

Solly leaned forward to where she was pointing. "Good grief," he said, "it's in Washington State on the West Coast."

Ross peered over his shoulder. "Is it far?"

Standing up, Solly stared blankly out of the dirty windows onto the winter street outside. "I'd guess the best part of three thousand miles," he said.

Chapter 4

Paulie

Paulie Ramos focused on the little group of wooden figures gathered around the crib and on the plastic doll that lay inside. She was only half listening to Pastor Smith recounting the story of the nativity, but simply watched as, one after another, a child would come from the congregation, stand in front of the scene and read from a scrap of paper.

The church was lit with candles—far more than was prudent—and its cavernous nave echoed to the joyous verses of "Oh Little Town of Bethlehem." For just a short while, it was possible to forget the Long Fall. Possible for some. Not for Sheriff Paulina Ramos. In her mind's eye she perceived the darkness outside and the evil things that hid within it.

She shook her head vigorously to wake herself. This was the first time in days that she'd simply sat still, allowing someone else to run the show. No one asking any questions of her, no decisions to make. It was so nice to sit here, enjoying the warmth and companionship of the church and participating in this group fantasy. After all, it couldn't hurt for a few minutes. Since that night, she'd tried to remember that life is nothing more than a succession of moments. It has a beginning and an inevitable end, and that sanity lay in the present. She just wished moments like this could last longer.

It was Sunday evening on December 20th and despite everything that had happened, the town was preparing itself for Christmas. For some it was about getting beyond what was sure to be a truly desperate time as thoughts turned inevitably to all those ghosts of Christmases Past gathered around the tree. Most of the adults, however, seemed determined that the children would have as good a festive season as was possible in the circumstances. There would be no game consoles, smartphones or tablets, but there would be scavenged bikes, skateboards, dolls and construction toys. This year, children would receive the sorts of gifts their grandparents would have recognized. But the gifts would be given by strangers and there was no masking the tragic background to this year's celebrations. Again, she saw the face of her daughter. Again, she felt the command she could not obey.

She jerked awake as a hand grabbed her elbow. "You were nodding," whispered the voice of Jon Graf.

"Sorry."

"Don't apologize, just get yourself some sleep tonight. Arbroath can cope without you for an eight hour stretch once in a while."

She turned to Graf and smiled. He'd been a rock in the weeks since he'd returned to town after burying his family. She'd served as a rookie alongside him when she'd first moved here and he'd played a large part in shaping her into the officer she was today. He was a man who believed that there were such things as right and wrong, black and white, good and bad, and it was for each person to decide which side of the line they stood on.

The final hymn washed over them, and they stood to leave. The thought of a warm bed and a decent night's sleep was now all that occupied Paulie's mind and she groaned inwardly as she heard the distinctive clippety-clip of the pastor's steel reinforced boots as he hurried to catch up.

"Did you enjoy the service, Sheriff?" he asked, his breath infused with the aroma of mulled wine.

Paulie filed between the rows of chairs toward the exit. "Yes, it was almost like a normal nativity. The children seemed to enjoy it."

"I think it's important to preserve traditions," Smith said. "They provide an anchor in turbulent times."

Graf let out a quiet snort, though the pastor didn't respond. Jon Graf had been one of the few townsfolk not to have fallen under Smith's spell. In fact, in Paulie's opinion, he went too far in his disdain for the man; so far, Smith had been nothing but good for the town. Her cop's instinct told her there was a lot more to him than the story he'd given, but they all had their secrets after all. In the first days and weeks, she'd waited for him to slip up and reveal his true purpose, but she was forced to believe that, whatever his past, he was here to help.

"I wonder if you'd be interested in a nightcap," Smith was saying.

"Sorry, Pastor, I'm not allowed out after dark. Especially in the company of strangers," Graf said, deadpan.

Paulie heard a sharp intake of breath from the pastor but kept her gaze on the approaching exit. "Oh, er, I'm afraid I was talking to..."

"Don't pay any attention to Jon, Pastor," she said. "He calls it a sense of humor. Truth to tell, I'm about ready to hit the sack. I nearly nodded off a couple of times during the ser—"

A cry went up from outside, and Paulie caught a glimpse of a man muscling his way against the congregation. "Sheriff!"

Deputy and former barista Mike Fessel ran up to her and pointed back the way he'd come.

"What is it, Mike?"

"A looter," he said as he caught his breath. "Two of Petrov's goons caught him stealing from the storeroom. Dragged him outside. Fixin' on hanging him."

Paulie broke into a run, pushing past the stragglers exiting the church. "Who's on duty?" she called over her shoulder.

"Marvin," Fessel responded. "But I ain't sure he's gonna do very much to stop it."

Paulie privately agreed with her deputy. Marvin Tucker had been the first volunteer to join the police force after the emergency had started. She'd recruited him on the principle that it was better to have him on her side than agitating against her. A former Gunnery Sargent in the Marines, he believed in simple justice swiftly delivered. That was about the only thing he and the much more measured Jon Graf agreed on.

She ran into the darkness with Fessel and Graf in her wake.

They were gathered around the monument to fallen soldiers in front of the department store that had been converted to house most of the people of the town. The monument was a large bronze cast crucifix and someone had swung a rope around the top.

A figure stood trembling on a wooden chair placed in front of the makeshift gallows as a baying crowd gathered around him, fists raised in anger.

Paulie groaned as she recognized the emaciated features. Charlie Givens had been the town layabout for years and if anyone hadn't deserved to survive that night it had to be him. So many good people had died and yet he had gone on to resume his career as a petty criminal and burden on society.

Tucker stood, shotgun in hand, facing Paulie as she ran up.

"Why haven't you put a stop to this?" she demanded.

The big man shrugged. "A stop to what, Sheriff? Seems to me that folks is just havin' a party. I suggest you let them be."

Paulie drew herself to her full height, which left her eyes at around the level of Marvin's chest. "Either get out of the way or hand back the badge, Deputy."

She could see muscles moving behind the messy non-regulation gray beard. He was angry, and she knew there wasn't much holding the rage at bay.

Fortunately, she'd quickly worked out that if there was one thing Marvin valued above being able to do exactly as he wanted, it was having a position of authority. Or, indeed, having an official role of any sort.

He reluctantly stood to one side as she, Fessel and the panting Jon Graf barged their way through to the front of the crowd.

To her surprise, she found Custer Petrov, owner of the department store, standing beside the chair, flanked by a pair of bald-headed grunts in fatigues whose names Paulie couldn't remember, though she knew they both ended in "-ov". It was rare indeed for the entrepreneur to get his hands dirty when he could act entirely through proxies such as the beef mountains standing alongside him.

"What are you doing, Custer?"

Petrov shrugged as if surprised at her question. "I bring a thief to justice," he responded, his soft voice barely audible over the noise of the crowd.

"In case you hadn't noticed, that's my job," Paulie responded, jabbing a finger at him as she fought to control her rage. She loathed the creep, but now was a time for a cool head.

"And yet you were not here. You were enjoying your little fantasies in the house of God, were you not?"

Paulie shook her head. "Not good enough. I had deputies on duty, you could have reported it to one of them."

"I did. Deputy Tucker was fully in agreement with my suggested action."

"He told you to string Givens up?"

Another little shrug. "Perhaps not quite in those words, no. But he did not object to my proposal."

"We have procedure, Petrov, even in these times."

"He was caught red handed stealing milk powder, there was no need for a trial. Do not our babies need this formula? Are our children not more important than this piece of filth." As he said this, he raised his voice, so the crowd could hear him. "And there is only one penalty for theft!"

Voices roared in response.

"Hang him!" some called.

"String him up!"

"Finish the scum!"

Paulie drew her Glock and pointed it to the heavens. Her shot brought instant silence to the mob.

"Now, just listen to me!" she called, wishing she had a few more inches in her legs so she could see over the crowd. She glanced over at Graf who, taking her meaning, drew a knife and slashed the rope from around the neck of Givens and pulled him, sobbing, off the chair.

Paulie climbed up and scanned the murmuring crowd. A couple dozen at most, but she could see others emerging from the department stores into the flickering light of the beacons used to light the nighttime square. She had only moments to quell the trouble before the extra onlookers poured gasoline on the flames.

"This isn't how we do things in this town. Justice denied anyone is justice denied everyone. It's my job to see due process carried out and when it's done, you have my promise that he will pay the price."

"He was caught stealin' out of the mouths of babes," called a voice.

"And I'll see justice is done, Jonas," Paulie responded. Jonas Fletcher was a farmer who'd been helping secure the stored produce of the surrounding farms and bring them into the center of town to feed the people through the winter.

"It ain't no kind of justice that scum like that get to live when so many good folk didn't. String him up!"

To Paulie's dismay, the call was taken up by others in the crowd and they began to press in. Givens gave a squeal of fear and crouched behind the reluctant protection of Jon Graf.

She'd lost them. They knew she wouldn't shoot on her own people, and they thirsted for vengeance. It was as if the transgression of Charlie Givens was the final straw and a red mist had descended on the town.

Givens called out as the muscled Russians grabbed him, and Paulie stumbled as she was pushed off the chair. Graf caught her. "Come on, we've got to get you out of here."

"No!" she called. If she lost control here, she would never regain it and that would be the beginning of the end for this oasis of civilization. But Graf pulled on her as the crowd pressed in on them.

She gazed up at Givens and saw him struggling ineffectually as the noose was retied around his neck. Her face burned with rage and panic as she was bundled sideways.

And then she heard the singing of children. The crowd quieted almost instantly.

"Once in Royal David's City,

Stood a lowly cattle shed,
Where a mother laid her baby..."

The crowd parted to reveal Pastor Smith striding across the square from the church followed by children bearing spirit lanterns. It was like a constellation of stars coming toward them, banishing the darkness.

By the time they reached the monument, the mob had almost entirely melted away.

The children spread out around the scene, some of them looking nervously up at the man standing there, but they kept singing and soon other townsfolk had flanked them and were joining in the song of peace.

Smith stood in front of the cross as if not noticing the criminal standing there. "As we near the day for celebrating the birth of our Savior," he said, "we do not forget his ending. But I'm sure you would not like these innocent children to witness your form of justice, Mr. Petrov."

Petrov stepped out from behind one of his guards and wagged a finger at Paulie. "You better keep those children around, Sheriff, or see that justice is done quickly. Now, I'm goin' back to the store to see nothing else is stolen."

He strode away, waving to the goons to follow and soon the square was deserted save for the police officers, the pastor and his flock. "I suggest you get him into a cell quickly," Smith said. "And then, perhaps, we can have that nightcap."

"That was a clever move," Paulie said, accepting a tumbler of whisky from Smith. "The singing cut through the ugly mood and the townsfolk knew they didn't want to be responsible for children seeing a lynching."

Smith sat down opposite her at the little table in the church kitchen. "I'm a clever man," he said, deploying the smile he thought was disarming.

"I don't know what got into them," she responded as she enjoyed the warmth spreading down her throat.

"They don't feel safe," Smith said. "I saw it time and again on the road—the less secure people feel, the less they're inclined to forgive others."

Paulie put down her glass and leaned back in her chair. "But they are safe. Or, at least, a lot safer than outside the barricade."

"You know that and so do I, but everything is relative. We both know we don't have the means to defend ourselves against a determined attack. I mean, what was the latest count on the weapons you've scavenged?"

Paulie shrugged. "I don't remember exact figures. Maybe a dozen shotguns, twice that number of handguns and a few assault rifles."

"And the militia that turned up shortly before I arrived—would it be enough to beat them off?"

She shook her head. "No. They had a couple of APCs mounted with machine guns and I don't doubt they had other grenades. It would only take a couple to blow open the gate in the barricade. I'm only surprised they haven't returned already."

"There are plenty of softer targets," Smith said as he drained his glass and winced. "But the better we do here, the more likely they'll be back."

"So, what's the answer?"

Smith smiled and, for a moment, the gentle, good humored, man of God disappeared and Paulie thought she glimpsed the steel that hid behind that grin. "We take our inspiration from the word of the Lord. Leviticus 24, verse 20."

Paulie watched as the pastor poured another round and lifted his glass.

"An eye for an eye," he said.

She raised her tumbler and touched it to his.

"Tooth for a tooth."

Chapter 5

Solly

Solly watched as the little girl leaned forward and tied the streamer to the top of the wall. She was sitting on the shoulders of an older child called Molly and laughed as her ride jigged around. The joy was infectious and Solly felt a smile spread across his face as they made their way around the room.

It was Christmas Eve, and the farmhouse was abuzz with anticipation. He, Janice, Arnold and Landon had twenty-four children in their charge, although the eldest of them, including Ross and Jaxon, had been forced to grow up quickly in the last weeks. Half of those children were under two years old, and the main concern of the adults was to make sure they were kept warm and fed as winter deepened around them. All but the youngest were being given boiled cow's milk provided by the small herd installed in one of the outer barns. Otherwise, their food stores were adequate for the winter and Solly refused to contemplate anything beyond that.

So, twenty-four children and one sick old woman. Solly had persuaded the librarian from Hagerstown to return with them to recuperate, but the woman had barely made it. In the darkness of the library, he hadn't noticed how frail she was, and they'd been reduced to carrying her by the time they'd arrived at the farmhouse. She'd been installed in what had once been a sitting room at the back of the house. Arnold had been using it as a bedroom up until then, since having a downstairs bathroom meant he didn't need to be carried up the stairs. But he'd given it up to her and had spent the nights by her bedside and the days snoozing in the armchair.

He'd also taken responsibility for giving the children the best possible Christmas the circumstances would allow. Somehow Arnold had ensured that every child old enough to appreciate it had a gift to open under the tree that dominated the main room of the farmhouse. Jaxon, it transpired, had played the role of Santa by keeping his eye open for suitable gifts during his many scavenging raids into Hagerstown accompanied by Ross and a couple of older children.

Solly had been given the task of providing the centerpiece of the meal on Christmas Day. He'd caught three geese in the creek and, through gritted teeth, had dispatched them one by one using the wood hatchet. It was these apparently humdrum activities of country life that reinforced how much had changed since the last time he'd celebrated this time of year. Solly Masters, a man who'd flirted with veganism, was now prepared to take a living thing and kill it without hesitation. He still hated doing it, but they had to eat and at least this way he was being accountable, truly understanding where his food came from for the first time in his life.

"Where are you going?" Janice said as he got up from the couch. Truth to tell, he'd been pretty comfortable sitting there with his arm around her, warm and dry on a wet winter's night. But he wouldn't be able to truly relax tomorrow, even for one day, if he hadn't settled on a plan of action. "Don't tell me, you're heading for the basement," she added, with a sigh as she watched him leave.

Solly navigated his way toward the basement door, dodging children burning off their excitement by running around the farmhouse playing tag. And this would be nothing compared with tomorrow. He smiled as he reached the door. It seemed to him that making sure the kids were happy for at least the next couple of days wasn't such a bad aim in life, but, right now, his bigger concern was to ensure their long-term safety.

The generator was running, so he switched the light on and shivered as a cold draught blew up the stairs. There, on the table, sat the safe containing the cylinder that had cost Jeremiah his life and beside it his pack, its contents spread across the surface.

The atlas he'd taken from the library lay open and he pulled up a stool to examine it. Behind him, he heard the creak of the basement door opening and footsteps on the stairs. "Hello Ross," he said without looking up, "did she send you after me?"

"No. I finished my chores, and you weren't around, so I came looking. You know, staring at the map won't make the journey any shorter."

"Neither will delaying it," Solly said.

"I dunno, but it'll be easier if we wait till spring, surely?"

Solly nodded. "I wish we could, but they probably know where we are."

"Who, Lee Corp?"

"Yeah. I don't reckon Jeremiah knew they could track the device—he thought it was just him and whoever he's working with. They might have picked up his trail some other way and followed him, but it seems more likely that they're using the same method to find the cylinder as he did."

Ross pulled up a stool and sat looking at the book. "And the last location was either here, when you pulled it out of the safe, or..."

"A couple of miles away where they ambushed Jeremiah. Either way, too close for comfort."

"But they can't track it now, can they?"

Solly shook his head and picked up a small black box. "I don't think so. Jeremiah's proximity alarm detects when the cylinder is nearby and, even though it's right here, it's not registering at all while it's in the safe. But anyone who comes looking for it will begin their search at the last known location."

"So what do we do? As soon as you get it out of the safe, they'll be able to find us. I don't reckon we'll get any further than Jeremiah did."

"You're right," Solly said. "The first job is to find a way to transport this while blocking its transmitter. Then, when we're a good distance away, we can deliberately remove it from its shielding for a while and hopefully take their attention away from here."

Ross contemplated this for a moment. "Making a fake trail? But how will we get away if they know where we are?"

"You're determined to come, then?"

"You promised."

Shrugging, Solly put the detector in Jeremiah's pack. "That was when I was planning to head to Texas, not on a two and a half thousand mile wild goose chase across the continent."

"So, you are going to take it to Arbroath, then?"

Solly sighed and turned around to face the boy. "I honestly don't know, Ross."

"I can't get my head around it."

"Well, let me put it this way. If we made it, we'll have traveled farther than Frodo did."

"But we're not going to walk it are we?"

Solly looked back at the map. "No. We'll have to car hop. Look at this," he pulled a small electric drill out of Jeremiah's pack. "He used this for draining cars. Judging by the oily smell, he only chose diesels, probably safer than gas. It's a lithium battery, so it keeps its charge for a long time, and I've had it plugged in when the generator's been running, but it's going to be hit and miss. And, when we're draining the fuel, we're vulnerable."

He stood up and pushed back the chair. "Well, we're not going to find all the answers sitting here and staring at the map. Let's go and see what's going on upstairs—it sounds like chaos." He smiled as he pointed up to the ceiling which was vibrating as children ran back and forth.

As they climbed the stairs, they heard the clanging of the warning bell.

Jaxon was outside the front door. "They're in the barn! Landon's on his way around there."

Solly ran to the armory, unlocked the door and pulled it open. Reluctantly, Solly and Janice had agreed to allow Landon to train Ross and Jaxon to use firearms but had insisted they stick to .22 caliber. Solly had found an old Marlin critter rifle in the farmhouse shed which he now handed to Ross, and Jaxon had unearthed a Ruger SR22 pistol which he'd taken personal responsibility for. Solly hated handing weapons to boys in their mid-teens, but he had no idea how many attackers there were, and they couldn't afford to be outgunned. And, after all, the raiders wouldn't know they were facing small caliber weapons.

They overtook Landon as he limped across the soggy field toward the main storage barn. Solly brushed sleet from his face and then pointed at a pickup truck parked outside the barn. "It's the gang that attacked you at Walmart," he said to Landon. "They're dangerous, so we have to take care. Come on."

Solly led them on a parabolic path, so they moved away from the barn before curving toward it again as they reached the other side. They hid in a small stand of trees at the edge of the field.

"They're not even bothering to keep a look out," Landon said as he rubbed life back into his leg.

Solly watched as figures ran back and forth from the barn to the pickup, loading the supplies he'd earmarked for the winter. He counted at least three of them, and they'd be carrying more powerful weapons than Ross and Jaxon's. "You wait here," he said to the boys. "Landon and I will get in close. Provide us with cover fire if things go badly."

"What's that supposed to mean?" Ross asked.

Landon turned to him. "If you see us a-runnin', shoot at them."

"I'm coming with you," Jaxon said, moving to follow them.

Solly grabbed his arm. "No! You wanted weapons, but you have to learn how to take orders. Wait here."

Jaxon's face tightened but, after a moment, he nodded. "Sure."

The two men crept along the line of trees until they were parallel with the entrance. A guard stood outside, scanning the lane and the road beyond it. Solly brought his Ruger to bear as Landon raised his shotgun. "Hey!" he called.

The guard spun around, unsure where the cry had come from.

"I've got you covered," Solly called. "Now take the stuff you've stolen from us back off the truck and leave it outside the barn."

Two other men dressed in black coats and pants with balaclavas were now standing beside the guard, their weapons sweeping the tree line.

One came to the front and called out, "I don't think so. You stole these here supplies and we're just stealin' from you. Now, unless you got a small army hid in them there bushes, I suggest you let us get on with our business and we might leave some for you. But if you try to get in our way, I might just have to go check what I might find in that farmhouse."

Solly's insides filled with ice. They were too far away for him to be certain of hitting any of the attackers, and as soon as he fired, he could expect instant and high caliber retaliation.

"I'm coming out," he called. "I want to talk."

The leader laughed out loud. "Sure, why not?" He turned to the others, and they resumed loading the sacks of grain and boxed supplies.

Solly stood up with his hands held high, allowing the Ruger to fall out of his grip. He began walking toward the barn. "I'm unarmed."

The man in black kept his handgun pointed at Solly as he approached. "That's close enough. Now, I guess you feel responsible for the folks in that farmhouse. Kids from the sound of it."

"I do. And they need food for the winter—food you're stealing."

The man shrugged dismissively. "You've been pretty resourceful to find this much, I reckon you can find more. Tell you what, we'll leave you a little and you can re-supply."

"There is no more," Solly responded.

"Well, I'm sure a man like you could use his imagination. We'll be back in four weeks, and we'll take half of what you gather."

"And what do we get?"

Again, the little shrug. "You get to survive, my friend."

"But you don't need this much, surely?"

The man's face spread into a smile. "Business is business," he said.

So, that was it. These scum would steal their food and then sell it. They'd probably try to sell it back to him. And given the efficiency and confidence they were showing, Solly suspected his wasn't the only farm they were extorting from.

"I suggest you leave us to finish what we're doing. It's cold out here," the man said.

With a sudden *crack*, splinters exploded from the corner of the barn. Something punched into Solly's cheek, but he ignored the pain, glanced at the leader of the bandits who had reeled backwards from the shot, pulled Mona's revolver from his inside pocket and pulled the trigger.

The bullet ripped through the man's neck, and he fell to the ground, his hands wrapped around his throat as he desperately tried to stem the flow.

One of the others emerged from the barn, his gun pointing directly at Solly who was late in bringing his own weapon up. Another crack and the attacker collapsed. Solly turned to see Jaxon and Ross running across the field, with Landon doing his best to join them.

A bullet zipped past his ear, and he took a dive. He could see feet on the other side of the pickup. He took aim and fired. The feet disappeared, and he saw the man rolling on the asphalt crying in pain.

The leader had gone quiet as Landon looked down at the second attacker. "He's dead. Lucky shot," he said. "I'll go check on the other one behind the truck."

Jaxon and Ross ran up and hugged him.

"Who took the pot shot?" he said.

Jaxon, looking a little sheepish, put his hand up. "Nice one."

"Landon got the other one," Ross said.

Solly let the boys go. "Now we just have to figure out what to do with the one I shot in the foot."

He turned to follow Landon around the car. There was a cry of fear followed by a bang and Solly found Landon standing over the last guard. "Problem solved," he said. "Merry Christmas."

Chapter 6

THE FARMHOUSE WAS FULL of the sounds of children playing and laughing, forgetting for a while the nightmares of the last weeks, yet Solly sat, hardly watching them, in his own personal cloud of despair.

He'd spent the previous afternoon burying the bandits in the woods that overlooked the farm. The children had been terrified by the shoot-out, and it had been all Janice could do to keep them contained in the house until it was over. When he'd returned to the farm, she'd thrown her arms around each of them in turn and let the children out of the main room.

Jaxon, Ross and Landon had helped drag the bodies across the field while Janice and Arnold kept the kids away from the windows. They'd spent a wet and miserable few hours digging a hole in the ground deep and wide enough for the purpose. Jaxon had surprised Solly by asking to say a few words over the freshly filled grave, and they'd trooped back to the house.

Solly had organized a watch schedule for the night as he was concerned that they might have been part of a larger gang, though he thought it more likely that they were working alone. The only good thing to come out of the affair was that they now had a pickup truck with a full tank of diesel.

Another screech went up as Janice announced that Santa was now ready to give out presents. She led them out of the living room, across the wide hall and through a door on the opposite side where, Solly knew, Arnold was dressed in red and white and wearing a straw beard.

Silence fell on the living room and Solly watched the children waiting in the hall as, one by one, they filed in. It touched his heart to witness such innocence in a broken world. What future did they have? Only what he and his generation could contrive to build out of the ashes. And even then, what of this second apocalypse that Khaled and Jeremiah had spoken of? Was all this struggling just a waste of time? Would they strive to get themselves back on their feet only to be struck down again?

"Penny for your thoughts?"

Solly had forgotten she was there. The old lady from the library had recovered enough to take the armchair in the corner that Arnold usually occupied. Her name was Agatha, though she liked the children to call her Miss Prism, and Janice had suggested she start teaching them after the holidays, if she chose to stay.

"I don't know," Solly said. "This seems so surreal, given what's happened."

She smiled and pointed at the hallway where the first of the children were sitting on the carpeted floor and opening their gifts. "They're lucky, especially the young ones. They know little of the past and nothing of the future. They miss their families, but here they have found a new one. It is quite an achievement, Mr. Masters. You should be proud."

"That's Janice and Arnold's doing," Solly said as he watched a young girl rip the wrapping paper from a box and squeal with delight as she pulled out a doll.

"You can't plant on shaky foundations. You have given them the security they need to build something wonderful here."

Solly leaned back into the couch and sighed. "Maybe, but not on my own."

"And now you're thinking you have to leave us," Agatha said.

"I'm torn in two," Solly responded, rubbing his eyes. "I feel as though I'm needed here and yet I do believe that I have a job to do that will take me away from here. And I still have to find my family."

Another squeal from the hallway. "May I give you a piece of advice? Call the adults together and have them help make the decision. But, for now, enjoy watching the children. Your gift to yourself can be to forget everything for a few hours."

THE COUNCIL OF WAR met on the following day. All the community's adults sat around the kitchen table, along with Ross and Jaxon who'd, by virtue of their conduct in recent days, have been given a field promotion to senior status.

The atlas lay on the table open at a double page showing the entire North American continent. A walnut sat over their current position and a brazil nut indicated roughly where Arbroath was on the northwestern coast. Even at this scale, it was obviously a vast distance. It looked hopeless.

After Solly had explained all that he knew about the cylinder, Janice reached out for his hand. "It seems to me that whatever the truth of that thing is, it can't stay here. Somehow Jeremiah was tracked by Lee Corp and that means they know, at the very least, that it was last located a couple of miles away."

"I don't understand why we assume they'll take it by force," Arnold said. "Couldn't we just offer it to them?"

Solly shook his head. "Jeremiah wasn't given the option. And you didn't see them in New York—they're paramilitaries and I don't want them anywhere near here."

"So, the cylinder has to leave here. But how can you get it away without having them come down on you immediately you take it out of the safe?" Janice asked.

"That's simple enough. I don't take it out of the safe. We've got a pickup outside that we need to get rid of, and I reckon we can get the safe into the back of it between us. Once I'm far enough away, I'll get it out and lay a false trail."

Arnold took a sip of his coffee and winced. "The question, then, is which direction to go in. Texas or Washington State."

"Why would he want to go to Texas?" Agatha asked.

Janice squeezed Solly's hand. "It's where his family lives."

"They're alive?"

"I don't know," Solly responded. "Probably not. But I need to know. I made a promise."

"Even assuming that they might still be alive, you wouldn't want to take the device anywhere near them, or you'd expose them to the same risks you're saving the children here from."

Solly sighed and ran his hands through his greasy hair. How long had it been since he'd washed properly? When had he last shaved? What had he become?

"I've got a suggestion," Ross said, hesitantly. "Why don't you take the cylinder far enough away to send them off on the wrong scent, then come back here and wait until the weather improves before deciding to head off across the country?"

There was a general murmuring of assent and encouragement.

"A good plan," Arnold said. "It means we only lose our Solly for a couple of weeks."

Agatha hemmed and hawed. "But a job put off is a job never finished, that's all I'm saying."

Solly smiled at Ross, but whatever he was going to say was cut off by the sound of a fist pounding on the door.

JANICE, JAXON AND ROSS called the all clear from their vantage points looking out over the farm in each direction. No new vehicles had appeared, and no one was moving.

The door shuddered again, and a male voice called out. "Anyone there?"

Landon took station behind the staircase and pointed his shotgun between the rails at the door. Solly had his handgun raised in his right hand as he turned the handle with his left. He gave a quick nod to Landon and yanked on the door.

A man stood in the doorway, leaning forward as if about to knock again. He stood up straight and raised both hands. He was wearing a heavy black coat with a scarf wrapped around his cheeks and a sodden woolly hat. "Thank heavens. It's you!" he said.

Solly brought his weapon to bear. "Who are you?"

"Neil!" Janice called. "Is it you?"

The man pulled his scarf from his face and stood, beaming, on the doorstep.

"Indeed. Now tell me, is Jeremiah dead?"

SOLLY, ROSS AND JANICE sat in the back parlor of the farmhouse while Neil Buchanan alternated between slurps of coffee and bites of a doorstop goose sandwich.

"This is amazing," he said, paying no heed to them.

There was little evidence of the well dressed and cleanly shaven man who'd met them when they'd arrived at the community in New Jersey. This Neil Buchanan had evidently been on the road for a few days, and he didn't look like a man used to deprivation of any sort.

Solly had quickly explained Jeremiah's death as Buchanan had refused to answer any other questions until he knew what had happened. The relief on his face had been obvious when Solly explained that he had the cylinder in the safe below the house.

"Is everything okay back home?" Janice asked.

"Hold on," Solly said, before Buchanan could answer. "Answer this first: how did you find us?"

Buchanan washed down the last of his sandwich with a final swig of coffee, then looked up at Solly and nodded. "That is a good question. But it's easily answered—I was given the same coordinates as Jeremiah. When he failed to check in, I was sent to find out what had happened."

"Sent by who?" Solly asked, though he knew the answer.

"Khaled—the man who gave you the device."

So that explained why they'd been welcomed into that community after they'd escaped New York. Neil was connected somehow to Khaled and had been forewarned.

"But the last we saw, he was being dragged off by Lee Corporation guards," Janice said. "Did he escape somehow?"

Buchanan gave a slight smile. "No, he didn't escape. Khaled works for the Lee Corporation, as do I."

Solly was on his feet in an instant, cursing that he'd left his revolver in the armory. Janice and Ross cried out in alarm.

"Don't misunderstand!" Buchanan called, raising his hands in supplication. "He and I, and some others, are employed by the Lee Corporation, but are working *against* its twisted aims. The device you call a cylinder is the single most important asset the corporation owns but, until just now, I believed that they didn't know it was even missing. Khaled had his suspicions and, when Jeremiah failed to report, we were both certain they were looking for it and, indeed, had found it. Thanks to you, we know that only one of those turned out to be the case. But time is now against us, Solly. The device must leave here in the morning. The future of humanity depends on it getting into the right hands."

THE SUN ROSE ON a blissfully blue sky as the group gathered around the big red pickup. Neil and Ross were coming with Solly, and they'd piled their packs into the back of the cab. The weapons of the raiders had been hidden in the basement of the farmhouse as a backup to the armory.

Despite Neil's insistence that they set off immediately, it had taken until midnight before Janice persuaded Solly that he had to go. He'd then spent some time with Landon, making certain in his own mind that the young man was up to the task of being chief protector of the farmhouse. Janice would be in charge, and she would be advised by Arnold. Solly went over his suggestions for security, including that Jaxon be fully trained in firearms, but that this should happen out of hearing of the farm.

He had his doubts, but there was at least a chance that this would be the making of Landon. He'd suffered as much as any of them but having responsibility for the safety of the farmhouse would provide a focus for his restless energy.

Solly had quick conversations with Arnold and Miss Prism, and then said goodbye to the children. He'd been surprised by their reaction. Many had dissolved into tears, some had begged him to stay, but he'd found it hardest to part from Jaxon. Solly knew that if he'd asked, Jaxon would have come with them, but he convinced the boy that his place was here, protecting the children that meant so much to him. In any case, he and Arnold's granddaughter Liana had become an item so there was that to keep him on the straight and narrow.

As Solly opened the driver's door of the pickup, Janice threw herself into his arms. They'd spent an all-too-brief time privately talking and holding each other after Solly had seen to everyone else and organized his possessions. He'd breathed in the scent of her hair and felt glad he'd showered in preparation for the journey. She'd never offered more intimacy, and he'd never asked but, in a different time and place, one where two compatible souls could get to know each other and fall in love in peace, he would certainly have trodden that path.

Solly felt a lump in his throat as he released her. For a moment, they held each other's gaze and then, quite suddenly, they leaned in and kissed. It was with tears in his eyes that he withdrew and got into the driver's seat.

Ross sat beside him on the center seat, also wiping his eyes. On his lap was a page ripped out of the atlas—much to Miss Prism's disgust—that showed the first part of the journey.

As they were about to go, Landon hobbled out of the barn carrying what looked like a pipe with a loop of string around one end and something metal stuck to the other. Solly opened his window and Landon showed him the contraption. "It's a bailer bucket," he said. "If you need to get fuel out of a gas station tank. Drop it down and it'll fill up, then this here valve stops the gas spilling. I've put a funnel in the trunk, so you're all set to go. Been working on it since our little chat."

Solly dropped the tube down behind his seat. "Thanks Landon. Where did you learn to make that?"

"Grandpappy had a well, and he used one of these to fetch the water out. I was just trying to find somethin' I could do to help, and I remembered the bailer bucket."

Solly shook Landon's hand. "Good man. I'll be back as soon as I can."

He turned the key, put the truck into drive and, without looking back, he drove down the lane toward the creek and the road that ran alongside it, trying desperately not to think about how many miles lay between him and returning to the place he now thought of as home.

Chapter 7

Paulie

"What's that?" Smith asked, pointing out of the car window to the right.

Paulie glanced across him. "It's the capitol building. I've often wondered if we should check it out, but I kinda expected to hear from them at some point."

They'd been forced off the main highway by what looked like a purpose built blockade that had since been abandoned so, rather than bypassing Olympia, they were driving through it. They were heading for the National Guard base in Seattle where she'd taken her basic training. She knew where the arms lockers were on the base and hoped that some of the more obscure ones might remain unopened. Then they'd have the means to defend themselves. But the journey had already taken far longer than they'd expected.

Paulie hadn't driven outside the city limits of Arbroath since the Long Fall. She'd listened to Smith's stories about his travels, but she'd only half believed him—partly because she knew he was holding plenty back about himself, but also because she didn't want to believe it. They were driving in convoy,

Paulie and Smith in the Cherokee, followed by Graf and Tucker in a delivery truck. She'd had reservations about bringing Tucker along after he'd come close to disobeying her orders the other night, but he was, after all, a former gunnery sergeant. He was also as hard as nails.

At first, they'd made decent progress, picking their way between the abandoned vehicles on route 12. Paulie had quickly learned not to look inside the cars and trucks, but rather to treat them as nothing more than obstacles to be navigated around. They'd seen no other living things except for carrion birds until they reached the small town of Monestano. As she looked down on it from the overpass, she could see movement. There was a small retail park with a McDonald's and a motel, and people gathered around a fire lit in a trash can. She saw them look up at the little convoy, pointing and then scurrying for cover.

The closer they got to Olympia, the harder it became to find a way through. In the end, she was forced to follow the truck as it barged a path through the scattered vehicles until, finally, they could go no further on the highway.

They passed along streets lined with low rise buildings before reaching the commercial area. A Korean grocery store with its windows blown inwards next to a burned-out Vietnamese restaurant and then, quite suddenly, as they reached an intersection, they found the road entirely blocked.

Two men, each armed with shotguns, walked up to Paulie's car.

"Who are you and where are you from?"

The speaker was an old man wrapped up in a large jacket and fur lined hat.

Paulie heard the quiet click as Smith flipped the safety on his M9. "I'm Sheriff Paulina Ramos from Arbroath. We're just passing through on our way to Seattle."

The old man peered into the car. "Just the two of you? So, who's your friend?"

Smith leaned over and held out his hand. "I'm Pastor Smith."

"You're a man of God? We have need of you. Come and have shelter with us for the night. My name is Jethro Thomas." He shook Smith's hand and then Paulie's. "And who's in the truck?"

"Two of my deputies," Paulie said. "We're heading to Seattle to see what supplies we can get."

Thomas looked doubtful. "Well, you know your own business, I'm sure. But I don't hear nothing good coming out of there. Anyway, you can leave your vehicles here and come inside. I'll set someone to watch them overnight."

Paulie glanced at Smith who nodded. The truth was that it solved the problem of where they were going to camp tonight. She hadn't wanted to stop in an urban area but neither did she want to go on driving for long after dark.

"We'll look after your weapons," Thomas said.

Paulie shook her head. "No way are we handing them over. One of us will stay here with them overnight."

THE COMMUNITY HERE WAS much smaller than in Arbroath and much less organized. No more than a hundred souls inhabited the hotel they'd commandeered and the safe area they'd created was no more than a couple of hundred yards across.

"We've done the best we can, but we got hit by bandits just as we were getting set up. Like fools, we thought they were the National Guard come to help us out, so we opened the gates and let them drive right in. Not that we could have stopped them even if we'd wanted to. Armed to the teeth, they were."

The image of the military convoy that had approached the barricade at Arbroath popped into her mind.

"We saw them, but they turned away."

The old man shook his head. "You were lucky—they took everything we had, and some of our younger menfolk even went off with them. We've been dreading them coming back. Mind you, we've hidden our food where they'll never find it if they come back again. Oh, here's Luigi."

They'd arrived at the center of a four-way intersection where a fire was burning, lighting up the square. A large middle-aged man walked toward them, then pulled Jethro aside. Paulie watched as the old man explained who they were, the other man's eyes darting back and forth between him and them.

After a few moments, he broke away and walked toward them with his hand outstretched. "Welcome to our community. My name is Luigi Napoli. Jethro is a trusting man to allow you in, but it seems you are not here to steal from us, and we are in no position to resist in any case."

Paulie took his hand, "Thank you. We' re grateful to have found somewhere safe to stop for the night."

Graf had stayed with the truck and Napoli seemed doubtful when he looked up into Marvin's bushy face, but his expression lifted when he met Smith. "Ah, thank the Lord. You have been sent to us in our time of need."

Paulie thought Smith gave a tiny sigh before responding.

"I am pleased to be here, Mr. Napoli. How may I be of service?"

Napoli took his arm and guided him to what had once been a women's clothing shop on the corner. "This is our makeshift chapel, Pastor. It would greatly comfort us if you would lead us in a service. We did not celebrate our Lord's birth as we would wish, but perhaps now we can make amends."

This time, Paulie was certain she'd seen it. Smith's shoulders sagged as if the burden of ministering to these people weighed him down. She watched as he was led away, and then noticed that Jethro was speaking to the others.

"... join us in our evening meal," he said, and headed toward a coffee bar. Candles filled the inside and Paulie's nose wrinkled at the bitter aroma of roasting beans. "Luigi is a clever man—he has adapted some charcoal barbecues, so we can cook and make coffee." He waved at the closed kitchen door.

The place was full of sullen people huddled together at tables eating rice. Paulie and Tucker found places on high stools at the bar. As they sat down, the kitchen door burst open and a figure emerged in a cloud of steam. It resolved into a beefy woman in chef's whites carrying a large saucepan. "Any more for any more?" she called.

"Over here, Moira," Jethro said. "Can we spare enough for another three visitors?"

The woman saw them for the first time. "Strangers, is it? But I can count, Jethro, and I only see two. Unless you're after another portion for yourse'n," she said in a broad Glaswegian accent.

"The other visitor is with Luigi. He's a priest, Moira. He's going to hold a Christmas service for us."

"Ach, that's all we need. And don't you go thinkin' I'm cookin' another Christmas dinner for the lot of you. We're fresh out of everythin' but rice, until you go shoppin' for me."

She ladled soup into four bowls and added cooked rice. "There, it's no exactly *haute cuisine* but it's fair good ballast for a cold night. I'll get you a coffee." Seconds later she returned with a drink and a bread roll for each of them. "Not many of these left either, Jethro."

Jethro sat beside them and watched them eat—a little too hungrily for Paulie's liking. "I'll go to the cache tomorrow, Moira. I'm sure we've got some of those part baked baguettes down there."

"Aye, well see you do, or you'll all be going hungry tomorrow night."

Paulie was enjoying the soup and rice so much she only noticed Smith's return when he sat beside her and began tucking in. "It's not much of a chapel," he said between slurps. "Just a cleared space with a cross made of two planks nailed together. He wants me to do the service tomorrow. I said we'll be leaving early, but this is going to delay us by a few hours at least. I can't really say no, can I?"

"Nope. And this trip is already taking a lot longer than I expected. We've gone barely fifty miles in a whole day. I feel twitchy being away from the place, especially after what happened on Sunday."

Smith tore into his roll with relish. "I don't think you need to worry too much. I reckon the lesson was learned. The mayor's keeping an eye on Petrov, but what can he do? He benefits as much as anyone else from having a safe and ordered community. I mean, can you imagine him trying to set up somewhere like this?"

Quite suddenly, he sat up straight and his hand darted down to his pocket. He turned to her, his face white. "Gotta go. Don't follow!"

He leaped off his seat and ran for the door as the heads of everyone in the coffee bar turned to watch.

She heard his voice coming from the makeshift chapel. She'd had no intention of obeying his order not to follow and had guessed he'd head there—where else could he have gone?

Paulie crept around the outside of the building, following the sound until she guessed she was on the other side of the window he was standing at.

"I don't care how desperate you are, we agreed you wouldn't contact me outside the schedule."

Silence fell, and she got the impression he was using some sort of two-way communication device and was listening to the response.

"How can they possibly have found out about it? How many of us knew about it?"

Pause.

"That's a pretty short list of suspects and you and I are both on it."

Pause.

"I'm in the field, you idiot!"

Pause.

"Yes, of course I've got it with me. I'm hardly going to leave it behind, am I?"

Pause.

"Do you know for certain it's been taken?"

Pause.

"In that case, I suggest we stick to the plan. Without the key, it's no use to them even if they do get their hands on it."

Pause.

"Yes, I know." Smith's voice softened, and he let out an audible sigh. "Look, what can I say? If it's been taken then there's nothing we can do to stop them, but at least they can't use it without the key."

Pause.

"No, neither can we. I'm sorry, my friend. Farewell."

Paulie was waiting for him as he left the shop. "Who are you?" she asked.

"I told you not to follow me."

Paulie shrugged. "Answer the question."

"If I tell you, then you'll be involved too. Nothing will be the same for you."

"Are you kidding me?" she yelled, gesturing around at the ruined town. "Now, you'll either tell me everything, or we leave you here—and don't imagine you'll be able to charm your way back into Arbroath."

He shook his head sadly. They both knew that in a popularity contest among the citizens of Arbroath, he'd win hands down. But Paulie was gambling that he wouldn't fancy making his way back along the roads on foot.

"Okay, you asked for it. Don't say I didn't give you fair warning," he said before leaning in to whisper. "My name is Scott Lee. My wife was Annabel Lee."

This was so left field it was entirely out of the stadium, and it took a couple of moments before it registered. "But you were the first to die."

He gave a wan smile. "Apparently not."

Khaled closed the connection and wiped his forehead as he sat back in his chair. Could he be wrong after all? Was it possible they didn't know about the device and their apprehension of Jeremiah had been a coincidence?

No. He didn't believe in coincidences. Neil had confirmed that the man he'd given it to in the first place, Solly Masters, had retrieved it from Jeremiah's pack having, it seemed, killed the two Lee Corporation operatives in the process. Mind you, Lee Corp's standards had slipped since the first wave. They seemed prepared to give a weapon and uniform to anyone who'd say the right words and pledge themselves to the company.

Of the many sins Khaled knew he'd committed over the past couple of years, breaking his word to Lee Corporation was the one he felt least guilty about. No, his sleep was wrecked by shame that he hadn't had the courage to begin preparations months before—when he could have saved a lot more people. He clung to the hope that he could make some amends by preventing the second wave which would see, at best, the survivors become slaves to Lee Corp and, at worst, the extinction of the human race.

The device represented the only chance of preventing that happening, but it had to get into the right hands and that depended on Neil and this man Solly. Neil Buchanon had been a facilities manager in a Lee Corp subsidiary who Khaled had befriended after a chance meeting at a company function. Khaled hadn't spent enough time around actual living people to become a good judge of character, but Buchanon exuded trust and charisma. He was also interested, at an amateur level, in the sorts of embedded systems that had been Khaled's life work. So, they'd become unlikely friends and when he learned the horrifying true nature of Lee Corp's plans, Neil was one of those he helped. It had been hard, very hard, to hide this, but he knew he had to try. He couldn't save the world, but he could save this man and his close family.

The door to his apartment slid open and two black suited security operatives ran inside.

"Hands away from the keyboard, Dr. Abdul, if you please."

Khaled swung around as the guards grabbed his arms. "What's going on, Commander?"

"We have finally caught up with the traitor who's been working against us all this time. Though with little enough effect, to be sure."

"I don't know what you mean!" Khaled cried, as his insides filled with ice.

Commander Chen leaned down so she could look directly into his eyes. "Don't lie!" she hissed. "We know enough to be sure you have betrayed us and what we don't know we will soon discover. Say goodbye to your apartment, Doctor. Your new accommodation is somewhat smaller and, I suspect, less to your liking."

Khaled shook his head. "There must be some mistake, I am loyal!"

She nodded at the guards who hauled him to his feet and began dragging him toward the door. A technician walked in and headed to his computer.

"This is doomsday," Khaled called and, at that, his computer screens shut down and the room filled with the stench of burning plastic.

"Quick, get the fire team in here now!" Chen called. She turned to Khaled, "You have just signed your death warrant," she spat.

Khaled dropped his head and allowed the security guards to drag him from the room.

Chapter 8

Bella

"Bella! Come quick!"

She found the old man in the living room of the beach house. He was crouching over something on the dining table. When he stood up, she could see that it was an old radio complete with physical knobs and buttons.

"... xico. Repeat. This is an automated announcement by the government of the independent states of Texas, Louisiana and New Mexico. To all citizens. There can be no recovery without security and so, in order to restore order and basic amenities, we ask that able-bodied citizens aged sixteen to forty-nine proceed to their nearest assembly point to enlist in our newly formed militia. Food, medical attention and shelter will be provided to enlistees and their immediate families. The list of muster points follows this message.

"My name is John Murphy, and this is the voice of your president. We are coming for you. God bless the Triple Star States of America. Here are the muster points for volunteers."

"Well, I'll be..." Al said as he put the pen down. "Maybe things are going to be put right after all.

Mind you, I guess anyone with a few guns could take over wherever the emergency broadcasts are made from and claim just about anything they like."

Bella slumped onto the couch. "I hope you're not thinking of enlisting—you're slightly out of their age range. But anyway, we can't go anywhere at the moment."

"How's the boy?"

"No better. The wound's looking pretty ugly and he's burning up."

Al switched off the radio as it began the announcement again and then shuffled over to sit beside her. "I'm sorry, *engel*. I must have left a splinter in the wound. Any luck with antibiotics?"

"No. Maddie's gone to see Silas, but I don't want my son's health to depend on that waster. And that doesn't solve the real problem—whatever's left in his leg. Oh Papa, what am I going to do?"

Al put his arm around his daughter. "Well, we must find some antibiotics first and then, my *liebling*, we will enlist him."

"What?"

"Didn't you hear? This new government is offering medical care to those who enlist."

She pulled away from him. "I don't want my son signing up for the militia of some illegitimate government!"

"If you have a better idea, I'm all ears," Al snapped. "Look, I don't like it, but there's at least a chance they'll have a proper surgeon who can sort him out for good. And then the boy can help restore order. Seems to me a few months of taking orders and hauling supplies is a small price to pay for saving his life."

Bella got up and walked across to the window. It faced the beach where a lone surfer was wading out to catch the next wave and two or three other figures were lying in the sand. Not a care in the world. She envied them. Jake had seemed to be recovering well after his injury, but once the antibiotics ran out, he went down with an infection quickly and now, just a few days later, he was completely bed ridden with a high temperature and swollen leg.

"Where's the nearest muster point?" she asked without turning around.

"San Antonio. Lackland Air Force Base."

"Good grief, that must be a couple of hundred miles away."

The old man came to stand beside her at the window. "Closer to three hundred is my guess, but I don't know where else we'll find a qualified surgeon or, at the very least, an army medic." He turned and grabbed her by the arms. "Come on, Isabella. Where's the *chutzpah* that's gotten you in so much trouble over the years? Three hundred miles, pah! If anyone can do it, it's my girl."

"I couldn't do it without you, Dad."

"Of course not, " he said with a smile, "You need someone along who knows which way up to hold a map."

Bella tied the scarf around her face again and took a deep breath. She'd decided that her best chance of finding antibiotics was to search the beach houses along the peninsula—the beach houses occupied by the dead. Rather than clear them in the first days,

Silas had simply declared them off limits and so they'd been left until now.

Crystal Beach was popular with the elderly, so it was a fair bet they'd have some medication stashed away, but Bella hadn't been lucky so far. She clenched her jaw and pushed the door open.

Even though she was holding her breath, she could still taste the stench in her nostrils. She ran in through the living room and flung the window wide open before leaning out and retching. She stood there for a few moments, her upper half in the fresh air, drawing oxygen into her lungs before turning to look at what lay on the couch. It had been human once, she knew, but now looked like something left over from Halloween. A shriveled form and a black stain.

She sucked in another lungful of fresh air and ran into the bedroom, pulling open the bedside drawers and throwing the contents on the bed. At last! She grabbed the box of amoxicillin and her hand brushed against something long and hard in the bed. She looked to her left to see a sunken head peering at her from beneath the blankets. She shrieked and ran, accidentally drawing a breath of poisoned air. Bella threw her hand over her mouth, exploded onto the veranda and vomited over the railings.

In her other hand, she held the box.

THE NEXT DAY, SHE put the final box of supplies in the back of the car and turned to see Jake struggling out with his arm around his grandfather's shoulders.

"Are you sure about this?" she asked as, with a groan, he heaved his injured leg in after him.

He looked up at her. "Do I have a choice?"

He shouldn't have been going anywhere except, in normal times, to the emergency room of the local hospital. His fever had relented a little and he could at least move now, but his skin was deathly pale.

"It'll be the making of you, son," Al said as he climbed into the front passenger seat. "You'll have a hand in bringing civilization back."

Bella had noticed that her father had become relentlessly upbeat since they'd decided to head to the airforce base. Jake had responded well to his enthusiasm, but she knew it was a shield Al had constructed to cloak his fear. Despite the chaotic nature of the community here, they'd felt safe in the beach house, and it had become their home.

Maddie climbed into the back of the car and slammed the door without a word. Worried though she was about her brother, she'd resented having to go with them. Bella, too, wished she could have left her daughter behind, but she simply couldn't trust Silas to keep her safe, especially after what had happened to Jake.

It was a hot day, and the windows were open as they pulled onto the main road and headed toward the 124. To their right, waves broke onto a deserted shore. The only movement they spotted was in the parking lot of a large hotel that faced the beach. A group stood beside a truck. It looked as though they were unloading supplies and Bella wondered whether there was a functioning community in that hotel or whether it was merely a meeting place for bandits.

The cars littering the road were now dusty and most had broken windows. Dark figures could be seen inside many of them, but it was easy enough to pick a way through. From time to time, they'd come across a section that had been cleared of cars and they'd occasionally spot people on the sidewalk, always in groups. No one walked alone, it seemed, even outside the cities.

Finally, they turned onto the main highway and from the light olives and yellows of the coast to the deep greens of south Texas. They passed a bait shop and a field of nodding donkeys. The road was more congested here and they were forced onto the grass more than once before going back to the highway. But there was no evidence of the new government until they saw a small shack by the side of the road. A man stood beside it and, when he saw them approach, he waved at them.

"Are you crazy?" Al hissed. "Don't stop!"

Bella ignored him, pulled the car into the side of the road and wound down the window.

"Howdy ma'am," the man said, leaning forward to see who was inside. "You look like a genuine family."

"We are. This is my father, and my son and daughter."

The man pushed his hat back to reveal the grizzled face of a veteran. He wore a faded camouflage jacket and an unkempt beard. "Wow, that's some kinda miracle. Me, I had no one to lose, so I guess we was both lucky. But here, I got some papers here 'cos you prob'ly don't know but we have ourselves a new government and Texas is a independent state again."

He handed over four leaflets, each folded in the center.

"We heard on the radio: Texas, Louisiana and New Mexico."

"Well sure, they're in it too. The TLX we're callin' it. But we're bossin' the others."

Bella cast her eyes down the leaflet. "So, nothing from the federal government?"

He shook his head. "Nothin' but promises. They can't barely get DC under control so when d'you think they'd be helpin' us folks out? No, we have to do it for ourselves, and the first thing is to get the military on the streets again. Gives folks comfort knowin' our guys have their backs." He paused for a moment and then pointed at Jake. "Your boy there, is he sick?"

"He's injured and needs medical attention. We're taking him to Lackland."

"He's gonna sign up? Good on you, son!" He reached through the car window, past Bella, and held out his hand to Jake who took it reluctantly.

Bella held her breath as the man pulled back again and stood beside the road saluting. "Godspeed to you all," he said.

"Have you seen many cars today?" Bella asked.

"A fair few, ma'am. A fair few."

She pulled away from the verge and watched in her rearview mirror as the man went back into the shack.

"How's the fuel?" Al said, leaning across and squinting at the car display.

"Fine," Bella responded, "I reckon we'll cover half the distance before we have to use your contraption."

Al sat back and smiled. He'd spent many hours over the past few days rigging up a fuel extractor that he was eager to test though, right now, he was enjoying the sensation of moving through the landscape on a clear road.

They were moving quickly along 124 and heading toward the intersection with 73 and then onto Route 10 taking them toward Houston. The plan was to bypass it on the south, although that meant going through Baytown. Bella wasn't sure they'd be able to resist checking on their family home, though she suspected it would be nothing more than a fire-blackened ruin.

"Slow down a bit, congestion ahead," Al said.

Bella huffed as she put her foot on the brake. Her father made for an aggravating passenger though, in truth, she'd been lost in thought and hadn't noticed that the number of abandoned cars on the road was increasing as they approached the junction with 73.

She slowed the car to walking pace as she steered it through the gaps that had been made between vehicles. She thought she could see people moving among the wreckage, but the way became suddenly clear and she put her foot down.

With a double bang, the car rocked, then jumped about as if she was driving off road.

"Blowout!" called Al.

Bella brought the car to a halt and jumped out. As she spun around, she looked directly into the barrel of a shotgun.

"Well hello," said a drawling voice. "You seem to be having a problem with your car. Perhaps we can help."

She looked up into a smiling face and then at the spike strip that ran across the road.

Bella watched as Al, Jake and Maddie were hauled out of the car and held at gunpoint by the side of the road.

"Careful, he's ill!" she called as Jake hobbled into place, sagging against the side of a vehicle.

"This here's a toll road," the man who'd spoken first said. "So, how are you goin' to pay?"

"Why didn't you just ask?" Bella snapped, her anger burning through her fear. "Why did you have to shred our tires?"

"Well, little lady, we've found that folks ain't entirely inclined to be cooperative if they can just drive away. Know what I mean?" He was a tall man in his thirties with a filthy yellow beard and a tattoo of a skull on his cheek.

He grabbed Bella by the arm and marched her around to the back of the car. The trunk was open, and another bandit was rifling through their possessions.

"What's this here?" he said.

"My dad made it for siphoning fuel," Bella said.

Skulls lifted it up. "Old man, did you make this?" he called, nodding to the thug who was holding him.

Al was brought around to stand beside Bella. "I did," he said.

"How does it work?"

"I'd be happy to show you, if you'd tell us what you intend to do with us."

Skulls regarded the old man thoughtfully. "Well, see here mister, we ain't murderers, if that's what you're thinkin'. We're traders and if you've got something to sell, we're inclined to buy."

"We haven't got anything other than what's in that trunk," Al said.

"You know what they say, knowledge is power. Are you an engineer, by any chance?"

Al shrugged. "I dabble. I fixed up a wind turbine. That's how we found out about the new government."

Skulls laughed. "New government? There ain't no law out here, old man. No law but us and these." He waved his shotgun.

"Seems to me you boys are behind the times and that might just get you into trouble before long."

The shotgun swung around so that it was inches from Al's nose.

"I thought you said you weren't murderers," Al said.

"Dad!" Bella hissed.

For a moment, the gun remained still but then, quite suddenly, it whipped away. "Well, you got spunk, I'll give you that," Skulls said, laughing again.

"Say, d'you reckon you could fix up some power for us. There's a turbine the other side of the car shop."

"Maybe I could," Al said. "We've got a job to do, seeing to my grandson. Once we've done that, we'll swing by, and I'll give you boys a hand."

"I don't reckon so. How about you get that turbine goin' and *then* we let you go on your way? Seems like a fair trade."

Al shook his head. "No can do. The boy needs urgent medical care."

"And where are you gonna get that? All the hospitals are shut down, old man!"

"Lackland Air Force Base," Al said simply. "There's a military hospital there that's open for business."

Skulls processed this for a few moments. "I don't reckon you're a liar, old man."

"The name's Al."

"But I ain't heard of that base, so it can't be around here."

"San Antonio."

"No way! We let you go, and we'll never see you again. No, you can stay—you'd just better work fast."

Al looked across to Bella. She could see him processing. Despite all the laughter and assurances, Skulls was dangerous, but there was no way they could agree to stay here. They had a few days of antibiotics—barely enough to get them to the base before the infection took hold again. To stay would be to condemn Jake.

"Let them go in a new car, with all their stuff," Al said, looking directly into Skulls's eyes. "And I'll stay."

"No!" Bella shrieked.

But Skulls smiled, spat in his hand and held it out. "You got yourself a deal old man. You got yourself a deal."

Chapter 9

Solly

Snow began to fall as they crawled northwest on the Dwight D. Eisenhower Highway. To Solly's eyes, little had changed since he'd last been on the roads except that the vehicles had begun to blend into the landscape as the greens and browns of dirt and algae accumulated. He didn't look at the decaying remnants of the people inside—the only good thing about the snow falling was that it offered the prospect of hiding the contents of the cars and trucks.

Their first target was Breezewood, PA, which would give them access to the Interstate 76 and 70 to take them westward. It was only sixty miles or so away, but Solly was under no illusion that they'd be able to cover that quickly.

Neil was snoozing in the seat next to him and Ross was between them, his head in a book. Solly steered the pickup slowly around a car on its side, blackened paintwork testimony to a violent end. To make a path, he was forced to push the end of the ruined car and the shunt woke Neil up.

"Where are we?"

"I just saw a sign for Indian Springs," Solly said.

"So, how far have we gotten?"

Solly shrugged. "Not far."

Neil grunted in frustration.

"Look, if you want an accurate fix, why don't you ask Google?" Solly said.

"Very funny. It's like going back to the Stone Age." He pulled the map sheet out of the glove box and squinted at it. "Could do with going to an eye doctor. I reckon I need a new reading prescription. Maybe fifteen miles. How long has that taken?"

Solly shrugged. "Does it matter? I guess a couple of hours. It's been slow going. We're lucky we haven't had to go off road yet."

"Breezewood, 36 miles," Ross said, pointing at the green sign as they rounded the latest stricken vehicle. "Will we get there before dark?"

"Look, I'm going as fast as I can—we can't risk getting stuck or damaging the truck," Solly said.

Ross settled back and resumed his reading. "I was only asking."

Solly sighed. "What's the book?"

"*The Fellowship of the Ring.* You said we were traveling farther than Frodo, but I've been reading for ages, and he hasn't gone anywhere yet. Just this inn in the neighboring village."

"I know how he feels," Solly responded as they crawled along the highway at barely more than walking pace.

They'd chosen Breezewood as their first stop off point because it had more than one gas station, so it offered the best chance of filling up the fuel cans in the bed of the truck.

The sky was darkening, and they'd been driving without lights, so they wouldn't be spotted, but it was now so gloomy they couldn't see far enough ahead. "Hey, what's that?" Solly asked.

A single lane had been cleared in the road, the lanes to either side were nose to tail with wreckage. At the end of the lane stood three men wrapped up against the cold who raised their weapons as the car was funneled toward them.

Solly wrapped his hand around his Ruger as his heart raced.

Neil brought the truck to a halt and wound down the window.

A face wrapped in a scarf against the cold looked inside. "Where are you folks headed?"

"We were hoping to get some fuel," Neil said, "There's a Shell station somewhere here, isn't there?"

The scarf was pulled down to reveal the face of a man of Asian descent with a stubbly beard. "The fuel belongs to the people of Breezewood, friend, so unless you've got something to trade for it, you better head off along the interstate. We're well enough armed to protect ourselves."

Solly's eyes drifted involuntarily toward the weapon pointing at them. It was an old hunting rifle. "We've got an assault rifle you could have," he said. "In exchange for some diesel."

The man glanced around the inside of the van.

"It's hidden," Solly said. "If you'll agree to let us fill up our cans, we'll hand it over."

The guard disappeared and Solly watched as he sauntered off to where a fire burned in an old oil drum. Two others stood there and, as they talked, each of them looked across at the truck.

"Amateurs," Neil said. "Just a group of residents trying to protect the only resource this place has got. They're lucky they didn't run into the previous owners of this pickup."

The man came back to the window. "We're gonna let you in, and then we'll take a look at that rifle you're offering and see if we can do a deal. Park in Sheetz," he said, pointing over his shoulder. "And no funny business. D'you hear me?"

It was like being threatened by a puppy. A puppy with a loaded weapon. Neil thanked the man and watched as he lifted the makeshift barrier before driving slowly through it.

A welcoming committee awaited them as they got out of the truck, weaponless hands held high. The sky was now almost dark, but two construction lamps illuminated the parking lot. So, they had power.

Around a dozen people awaited them. Half had weapons pointed at the newcomers, and a black woman was the first to come forward. "We welcome you in peace," she said, holding out a hand. "My name is Hanna."

"A funny kind of peace that involves pointing guns at us," Solly responded, returning the handshake and giving his name.

She smiled and gestured around the forecourt. "We are peaceful, but not entirely naïve, Mr. Masters. We would not have survived these past weeks had we been so. George believes you are good folk, so we have admitted you. We mean you no harm, but if you wish us to share our fuel with you, then you must give us something we need in return."

Solly introduced the others and, while they were shaking hands, went around to the back of the truck and rolled back the cover, taking care to move slowly and deliberately, aware that he was in the sights of several shooters.

He came out holding one of the weapons they'd taken from the former owners of the pickup.

"Here, this is what we have to offer," he said, removing the magazine and stepping forward.

"Carl, what d'you say?" Hanna said.

A nondescript man wearing a trimmed mustache lowered his weapon and stood beside her. He took the weapon from Solly and examined it.

"M16, standard issue. Good condition, bit of an antique. Military's been using carbines for years."

"Will it improve our ability to defend ourselves?" Hanna asked.

Carl nodded with thinly veiled enthusiasm. "Oh yeah, it sure will. As long as these fellas've got some rounds to go with it."

"Worth a dip in our pond?"

He looked from her to Solly and the others, weighing them up.

"Carl, we're doing a trade here, that is all—do you understand?" Hanna said, turning to face him. "It's a matter of deal or no deal, those are the only two options on the table."

His eyes swung back to Hanna, and, for a moment, he seemed prepared to defy her, then he looked back at Solly and nodded. "Deal."

"Good, now you have four jerry cans to fill? So that's about twenty gallons. Well, the rifle and a full magazine buys you ten gallons, the other ten depends on how much more ammunition you have to sell, or anything else you want to trade. Now, it's too late to dispense the fuel tonight, so why don't you make yourselves at home? There's a Day's Inn right next door. The ground floor has been cleared, so feel free to settle in. You can sleep safely tonight."

THEY FOUND A ROOM that looked out onto the hotel parking lot and left the truck right outside the window.

Solly hoisted his pack onto the bed and sat down with a sigh. It had taken an entire day to cover the fifty miles to Breezewood. At this rate, it would take the best part of a year to get to Arbroath.

"Do you trust them?" Ross asked as he dropped his backpack on the floor and looked out the window. Flecks of snow appeared in the light of the candle set on the sill, but the only other movement came from the shadows walking across the communal fire at the roadblock.

"Hanna seems okay," Solly said, "but we can't take any chances, so one of us will have to keep an eye on the truck."

Neil was busying himself setting up the camping stove. "I wonder how she keeps everyone in line. That man who took the weapon—what was his name?"

"Carl," Ross said.

"Yeah, Carl. He's a troublemaker or I've never met one, but even he put up and shut up when she spoke."

The room filled with the aroma of baked beans, and he busied himself chopping up some hot dog sausages before stirring them in.

"Here," he said as he handed a bowl to Solly. "Not exactly Gordon Ramsay, but it'll keep us full for the night."

They lit candles and Solly sank into the armchair while Ross and Neil sat on the pull-out couch. One of the silver linings to this cloud—insignificant though it might seem—was that he appreciated food far more than he'd ever done before. It had transformed from being either a necessary evil that interrupted work or an excuse for overindulgence into a basic requirement, the fuel that would get his body and mind through another day.

"You know what this needs?" he said as he spooned in another mouthful. "Some grated cheese. What I'd give right now for a block of parmesan."

"Sorry, Sol," Ross said, "I don't think the restaurant can stretch to that. Maybe we should look out for some on our travels."

They ate together in a silence only broken by the sounds men make when vigorously consuming food with no women around. The beans had been replaced on top of the stove by coffee grounds and Neil poured the dark liquid into each mug before handing it to them.

"You know what," Solly said. "If there's one thing I've learned from this nightmare, it's to appreciate brief moments of happiness. And I'm enjoying this. Here's to you both."

They touched mugs and slurped down their coffee.

"Can we have a story?" Ross said. "You know, a fireside tale? Something creepy."

Neil stifled a grim chuckle.

"What? Have you got a good one?"

"No, I was just thinking that we're living in a pretty creepy story right now," he replied, before pausing for a moment. "Well, I suppose I could tell you the tale of Annabel Lee."

"It was many and many a year ago,
In a kingdom by the sea,
That a maiden there lived whom you may know,
By the name of Annabel Lee," Solly chanted.

"Edgar Allan Poe?" Neil said.

"The Stevie Nicks version."

"Well, sadly the real life Annabel Lee wasn't quite the angelic love bird of the poem, though she certainly took her name from it. Tell me, Ross, what do you know of her?"

Ross shrugged, though delighted to be asked. "I guess I know what everyone does. She was the genius who created the Bones implants. Saved millions of lives."

"Her face was on the cover of *Time* magazine more times than anyone in history," Solly said. "She was like Steve Jobs times ten. Most people saw her as a savior, others as a wolf in sheep's clothing—not everyone liked the idea of the implants."

Neil nodded. "I think she began with the best of intentions. She was born in India, you know. Her mother was Chinese and her father English, but she was educated in the US as well as the UK, so she had a very global viewpoint. She was born Annabel Jones, but she took her mother's surname when her parents divorced as she blamed her father's infidelity for the break up. And it meant she had the same name as that Poe character—I think that influenced her more than most people imagine."

"Well, this is all fascinating, but where's the creepy story?" Ross asked.

Neil smiled, took a bottle from his pack and poured a little liquor into each mug before saluting them again. "Well, I won't bore you with the details of how she used her time in India to focus her innate genius on solving health problems. She met her future husband when she was studying for her doctorate at MIT."

"Scott Lee was brilliant in his own right," Solly said as Neil drew breath. "He's credited with developing some of the most advanced algorithms in the world. I've worked on projects that used them. Amazing."

Neil nodded. "Indeed, an underrated genius. But Annabel became the mast he tied himself to, so he poured his expertise into helping her realize her dream of self-diagnosing implants that could save lives both as emergency resuscitation devices and by providing early warning of diseases and conditions. Brilliant concept. And then the medical insurers got wind of what she was doing, and they became mandatory almost overnight."

"Don't I know it," Solly said. "When I started working at IncaTech the job offer was conditional on getting the implants—and on my wife and children having it. Paid for by the insurers, but I wasn't happy. Lots of people held out to begin with, but the premiums were so much lower, pretty much everyone got onboard in the end. And then, when I went to work at Taylor and Ritchie, we had to have this new upgraded Chinese model fitted."

Neil leaned in, as if the walls might have ears. "So, if you'd gone through all that, how would you feel if you got a disease that the Bones didn't pick up until it was too late? A disease that's typical of the poorer countries of the world where there's no commercial case for early diagnosis?"

"I'd be pretty cheesed off," Solly said.

"How much angrier would you be if you'd devoted your life to building a device that then fails to save yours?"

Solly lowered his mug, his mouth dropping open. "Are you saying that's what happened to Lee?"

"Guys, what's going on outside?" Ross called out.

Glass exploded inwards as a hail of bullets punched holes in the opposite wall. They dropped instantly and Solly desperately searched for his weapon. Ross crawled under the bed as rounds continued to spit into the room, shattering mirrors and splintering door frames. He came back with Solly's Ruger and pressed it into his hands. Solly flipped over and pushed at Neil, but there was no response.

"Neil!" he hissed as the firing stopped. He pushed harder and Buchanan rolled onto his back, his sightless eyes staring upwards.

The barrel of a gun appeared through the window.

"Reckon we got 'em," hissed a voice from outside.

Solly's mind filled with a red mist as he recognized Carl. Solly and Ross were right under the window, crouched in a fetal position. Solly nodded to him hoping he'd understand and then, in one swift movement, he grabbed the barrel of the shotgun with one hand and brought his weapon up with the other. The man's eyes widened for an instant before Solly pulled the trigger and he dropped.

It wasn't Carl. He was standing to one side, out of harm's way, or so he thought, but now he brought his rifle up and was leveling before Solly could react when a shot rang out and he fell sideways, blood jetting from his shoulder.

"Put your weapons down!" Hanna's voice called from out of the darkness. "Put them down! There's a half dozen of us with you in our sights right now, so drop them."

Solly sighed, then knelt beside Neil, feeling his throat thicken and water forming in the corners of his eyes.

He barely heard Hanna call out from the other side of the ruined window, "Looks as though we'll be having a hanging."

Chapter 10

Bella

Bella had never felt so alone. It had been more than 36 hours since her father had chosen to stay with Skulls and his gang, and she couldn't help but wonder whether he was still alive. Surely, he wouldn't be able to keep up the pretense that he was an engineer for long? He was a clever man and good with his hands, but it was a long way from fixing the domestic wind turbine on the beach house to doing the same for a commercial setup. Soon enough, he would be exposed, and Skulls would exact his revenge.

But it was the loneliness that was crushing her. She'd been driving through a desolate landscape of abandoned vehicles and burned out houses with a sick son and a daughter who had said barely a dozen words since her grandfather had left. It was as if Maddie blamed her for grandpa's sacrifice. Well, maybe she was right.

The journey itself had also taken its toll. They'd stopped at their old house in Baytown to find it a burned out ruin and all three of them had spent longer than they should have done sobbing at this most personal wound to their shared history. Now they were homeless, unless they could call the beach house home, and the only thing on Bella's mind was getting Jake the medical attention he needed before it was too late. So, she skirted around Houston to the south, before heading for I-10. She'd briefly wondered why the governor hadn't chosen Houston to be a muster point for his new militia, it would certainly have been more convenient if he had, but, as she skimmed the outskirts of the city, all she could see was a pall of smoke hanging over it. It was as if it had been burned as thoroughly as their home.

When they finally reached the interstate, it was impassable for many miles, so she shadowed it on smaller roads and dusty tracks until she could see gaps appearing between the vehicles. The east bound side cleared first, so she hopped onto the road and drove against the direction of the traffic, weaving around the wreckage and, once or twice, was forced to leave again only to pick it up at the next intersection.

They saw other people from time to time. For a couple of hours, they were part of an unofficial convoy of three cars heading west until the other two, on missions of their own, turned off the interstate and headed into the country.

It didn't help matters that she was driving an unfamiliar car. Rather than replace the tires on her SUV, Skulls had told them to pick a car from the dealership and it didn't sell many larger cars. She was, in the end, forced to choose a Toyota Land Cruiser with a manual shift and she'd entertained Skulls and his cronies by kangarooing along the road. By sheer luck, however, it had an almost full fuel tank, so they stood a fair chance of getting to San Antonio without needing to find more—as long as they weren't forced to abandon the car along the way.

"Look!" Jake said. It was his turn to sit in the front and he jabbed a finger at the windscreen.

At first, she thought it was a regular road sign, but over the metal frame hung a white banner. A message had been hand painted with care onto it:

Welcome to the Free States of Texas, Louisiana & New Mexico.

"So, it is a thing," Bella muttered. Relief flooded her body. Part of her had wondered whether they weren't following a phantom across the country, a sort of Shangri La that could be sought for, but never found.

As they approached the sign, the road suddenly cleared from side to side and there, a few yards inside this newly declared border, stood a military checkpoint.

Bella slowed the car gently as she approached it before bringing it to a halt. Three men in military uniform stood behind the barrier, their guns trained directly at her, while a fourth approached the car, gesturing for her to wind down the window.

"Good day, ma'am," he said in a broad south Texan accent. He was wearing a modified Texas National Guard uniform—the name strip had been torn off and replaced with a plastic badge. "I'm Corporal Demers. There are three of you in the vehicle?"

"Yes, these are my son and daughter."

His eyes opened wide. "Your actual flesh and blood?"

"I've been very lucky," Bella said.

"It's a God given miracle," Demers said, smiling. "But what's your business here?"

"I'm taking my son to Lackland Air Force base to enlist."

His smile widened. "Well, good for you. But your boy don't look too healthy."

"He was injured," Bella responded. "We're hoping the army medics can help us."

"Sure they will. Okay, you'll have to give me your names to go on this here form, then I'll give you a docket to put in your window so's the other checkpoints will let you pass. It'll also get you a place for the night."

This was welcome news as dusk was only an hour away. She'd planned to sleep in the car, but the thought of a safe bed threatened to overwhelm any sense of caution.

"'Cos rule number one is 'Respect the curfew.' Dusk till dawn, no folks are to be out. Don't you forget it, 'cos it's a shoot on sight policy. Can't be too careful till security is totally established."

Bella gave her details and watched as the corporal filled out the form with the slow and deliberate care of a man new to the task. She had little experience of the military, but she'd be prepared to bet that six weeks ago Corporal Demers had been earning his living in an entirely different way.

"Here you go," he said, handing over a piece of paper with a crudely drawn symbol on it. "That should see you right. Now, head along the road and the guys at the next checkpoint will point you in the right direction."

THEY PULLED AWAY FROM the checkpoint as the barrier was raised and Bella watched through the rearview mirror as it closed again like the shutting of a door. She couldn't explain why, but it gave her the creeps, but her mood soon lightened as they drove into another world.

There were no abandoned cars on this side of the border. In fact, it was only the lack of traffic that gave any hint to the truth that these weren't normal times. They had less than an hour's daylight left, but she could see no sign of strife anywhere on the flat landscape to either side of the highway. Leafless bushes marched alongside the road and beyond she could glimpse wide tussocky expanses of scrub dotted with small crops of trees.

Finally, as she was beginning to worry about it becoming dark before they found shelter, she saw the lights of another checkpoint ahead.

A clean shaved young man looked in through the side window. "Ma'am this ticket says you're to be found housing. Please take the slip to the right and follow the track until you reach a house on the left, they'll take you in."

Bella thanked him and was going to pull away when he said, "Did the guards at the other checkpoint search the car?"

"What for?"

"Weapons, primarily."

There was no sense lying. "No."

The soldier straightened up and gestured to his comrades. Bella thought she heard the word "amateurs" under his breath.

"Would you please open the trunk," he said aloud.

Bella got out and padded around.

"We will need to search you and your companions," he said as he riffled through their belongings.

Jake groaned as they helped him out of the car.

"What's the problem with him?" the first guard said as he spent slightly longer than was necessary patting Bella down.

"He's got a leg injury. It's infected and we're nearly out of antibiotics."

The guards straightened up. "You'd best set off for the base first thing in the morning. It might take a while to get you processed."

He conferred with the other guards and showed Bella a plastic crate containing their guns.

"Here is a list of the weapons we have confiscated. They will be added to the state armory."

"We can't have them back?" Bella asked, horrified.

He shook his head. "You won't need them. You're inside a safe enclave."

"What about the Second Amendment?"

The guard guided her back into the driver's seat. "We have a new constitution, ma'am. Only members of the armed forces or the militia are permitted to carry weapons. Now, head to the right and follow the track. Have a good evening."

Bella started the car in a daze and headed in the direction he'd indicated. She'd never been a vocal fan of guns, but the right to self-defense was ingrained in the souls of most Texans and the idea that they'd give that up was impossible to process. Except when you considered that nineteen out of twenty were now dead. History had shown time and again that a small determined group can quickly come to dominate a much larger population if they act swiftly and decisively.

The lane meandered off to the right, on one side bordered by a huge paddock and on the other by scrub. Then a large white house emerged from the left and she swung into the dusty drive. Before she'd brought the car to a halt, a man appeared on the veranda and strode out to meet them.

"You must be newcomers," he said, his hand held out in greeting. "Come inside quickly, it is nearly time for curfew."

He was a big, bearded man wearing denims and a thick woolen sweater.

Jake moaned as his leg gave way.

"I will help the boy," the man said. "You can bring your bags."

Bella and Maddie followed him up the steps to the front door which stood wide open. Lights blazed from within, and a smiling woman took Bella's bag and led her through the house.

"My name is Ethan Calder," the man said after he'd helped Jake onto the bed. "This is my wife Alice, and you are welcome in our home. You will find a washroom through there and, once you've freshened up a little, please join us in the kitchen for the evening meal. We'll keep it warming until you're ready."

"Please don't wait for us. Go ahead and eat," Bella said.

The big man shook his shaggy head. "We have the honor of welcoming newcomers who need shelter for the night, not knowing our laws, and so we will wait for you." He turned and followed his wife out of the room.

"I feel as though I'm in an episode of *Westworld*," Maddie said as she looked around the room. "I mean, it seems too good to be true, doesn't it? Or is it me?"

Bella put her arm around her daughter's shoulders and was relieved that she didn't resist. "No, I feel it too, darling. I've felt it ever since we crossed the border, and even more so when they took our guns. But we've got no choice but to play along—nothing's more important than Jake getting the help he needs. We can figure the rest of it out from there."

A SHOWER—A GENUINE, ACTUAL shower powered by an electric pump—and a change of clothes had brightened the moods of both Bella and Maddie. Examining Jake's wound, on the other hand, only made the urgency of their task all the more obvious and her heart broke as she watched her son struggle into the shower. Frankly, she'd do a deal with the devil himself to get him seen to and cured.

Ethan sat at the table with a young girl he introduced as his daughter, Margaret, while Alice busied herself at the stove. The kitchen was filled with the rich aroma of a beef stew.

"Please, sit," Ethan said, indicating three seats on the opposite side of the table.

Bella watched, her mouth watering, as Alice ladled the stew into wide bowls and handed one to each of them.

"Tell me, Ethan," she said, forcing her attention away from the food while Alice piled on fresh vegetables, "how are things here, in, what do you call it?"

"Officially we live in the Free States of Texas, Louisiana and New Mexico, but most call it the TLX, even the governor."

"So, you're not part of the USA anymore?" Jake asked.

Ethan gave a shrug. "I think most of us think of ourselves as Americans still, but the USA as a political unit ceased to exist six weeks ago and we have been forced to take matters into our own hands. Though, I take no credit for that. I am a humble follower. But here, let us eat before we talk. Shall I say grace?"

The stew was delicious. It was as if Bella's taste buds had been on vacation and were finally being given something worth eating for its own sake as much as its nutritional value.

There was even a decent Texan Chardonnay to go with it, but Bella didn't want to let Ethan off the hook so, when they left the table to sit in the living room, she brought the subject up again.

"What do you know of the governor?"

Ethan's face darkened just a little at the change in subject—he'd been holding forth on the farming prospects for the next year.

"I know he's a good man. Used to work in the Texas government. He brought together the surviving leaders and... " he gestured around as if his living room was evidence in itself, "the result is peace and people getting fed. I don't hear no complaints."

Bella opted to drop the topic. She was puzzled by Ethan's defensive reaction whenever she asked anything, so she switched onto safer ground. "We do have one thing in common; our families survived. I'm certainly thankful for that."

Ethan seemed to relax at this. "We sure are lucky. Now, why don't you head along to bed—you want to be up and on the road early tomorrow to get that boy seen to."

Though surprised at this abrupt dismissal, Bella was exhausted and welcomed the idea of sleeping in a real bed again. Two nights in the car had done her back no favors.

As they were going into their room, Bella heard little Margaret's voice behind them.

"Oh, go on then," he said in reply. "But don't go bothering them."

Margaret slipped past her father and ran up the corridor, a cuddly toy swinging from her arms.

"I've got this for Maddie," she called as she came into the room. "Here, I thought you might want something to cuddle tonight."

The little girl turned to go out again as Ethan's footsteps approached. As she passed Bella, she quickly leaned up and whispered in her ear.

"He ain't my daddy and she ain't my mommy. I gotta pretend like we're family, but we ain't. Watch your girl."

And then she was gone.

Chapter 11

Paulie

Paulie scanned the compound from the fourth floor of a ruined building and sighed. "We're too late."

Figures in military uniforms strode back and forth across a cracked concrete landscape of rusty containers and military vehicles.

"Looks as though it's pretty organized down there," the man she'd known as Pastor Smith said.

They'd barely spoken since the night she'd overheard his radioed conversation with his contact within the Lee Corporation. At first, she'd refused to believe him. How could he possibly be Annabel Lee's husband, the man whose death in front of the world's cameras had signaled the beginning of the Long Fall?

Her mind rejected the possibility outright, but her heart told her it was the truth. He said he'd become aware of his wife's intentions too late to prevent them being realized, so he'd injected himself with a paralyzing agent, making it appear he'd died instantly. His conspirators then removed his body, using the unfolding chaos of that night to shield their movements. He was taken to a small community to the south where he convalesced and set out on his mission in the West.

He wouldn't reveal what this mission entailed, despite Paulie's dogged questioning, and this lack of honesty, along with the fact that he'd been fooling them ever since he first walked into Arbroath, had been enough to build a wall between them. Though she did have a sneaky admiration for the sheer balls it took to impersonate a priest using nothing more than a Bible and Book of Common Prayer he'd found on his long journey, along with memories of a Catholic upbringing in the UK. That he was British was another surprise, but he'd been in the US for long enough to be able to adopt a completely authentic east coast accent.

She'd reluctantly agreed to keep his identity a secret for now as long as he kept to his side of the bargain and continued to provide the spiritual support the people of Arbroath needed, at least until he completed his mission. Whatever that was.

Paulie peeked out of the window again. She'd expected the armory to have been raided in the preceding weeks, but she'd hoped to find some of the better hidden caches untouched. She'd also thought it unlikely that anyone would think to drive away with the military transport vehicles and APCs. She'd been wrong about that too as only a couple of rusting specialist trucks remained on the other side of the razor wire.

She slid down the wall and took the cup of coffee from Marvin, who'd set up a camping stove in the corner. Beyond him, Paulie could see the first of a row of steel lockers that ran around a central landing. Most had been broken into at some point since the Long Fall began and the personal possessions stored there stolen. How pointless it all was, she thought. Just like this mission.

Then the floor began vibrating. "Something's coming," Lee said.

Paulie got up onto her haunches and looked out over the window sill. A small convoy of military vehicles was approaching from the left. Several trucks followed two tanks. Ahead of them all was a jeep. "I know him!" Paulie gasped. "It's the leader of those bandits who threatened Arbroath."

"Good grief," Lee responded, "So do I. He works for the Lee Corporation."

The gates swung open, and the convoy trundled into the compound. The leader waved and jumped down from the jeep, receiving cheers from the soldiers. Paulie watched as, after some handshaking and backslapping, he shepherded them to the rear of the convoy—the trucks had come to a halt with their rear doors facing where Paulie and the others were. He swung open the doors of the first and the cheer went up again. Between the bobbing heads of the onlookers, she could see what looked like boxes of food, enough to feed an army.

He moved along to the second one and, this time, two armed soldiers jumped down first. Paulie squinted into the dark interior of the truck and then gasped. "They've got people in there!"

Again, the cheer went up and Paulie wondered whether they had rescued these people, but one look at the first person to walk down the steps banished that thought. It was a youngish woman wearing stained clothes. Her body was stooping, like a trapped animal, and her hands were tied. A man followed her. His face was bruised and the t-shirt she could see beneath his jacket was splashed with blood. He was also bound around the wrists and two guards manhandled him, so he stood beside the woman alongside the truck.

Paulie was unable to glance away from the procession of men, women and children who hesitantly climbed down the steps and into the light, only to be lined up next to the others. It was like a scene out of *Schindler's List*.

"The most valuable resource in this new world is going to be manpower," Lee said. "How big is this base?"

"Big enough to hide a small army. Who is their leader?"

Scott Lee continued watching the sad parade. "Lad Melua. He was appointed head of security for the Seattle building. Born in one of the old Soviet states but came over as a child. Brutal."

"What was the Lee Corporation doing hiring thugs like that? It's a tech company, isn't it?"

He settled back down to take a swig of his coffee. "Technology is expensive and has to be protected. Anyway, this particular company had a mission or, at least, I thought it did."

"What do you mean?"

"Well, clearly it had a mission, it just wasn't the one I thought I'd signed up for. The alleviation of suffering; that was my calling. And being given a good cause to continue my research."

The guards herded the last of the people into a low building behind the loading bay, and Paulie sat back down to finish her coffee.

"Ain't there nothin' we can do?" Tucker said, withdrawing from the window. "Them poor folks. It ain't right. I swore an oath to protect the constitution and there ain't nothin' in there about treating people like cattle."

Paulie tried to hide her surprise at this compassion in someone who, only days ago, had been willing to string up a petty thief.

"I know what you're thinkin'," he said, "but he was a criminal and caught in the act. These are probably just innocent folks. Could have been us if we hadn't stood together and I figure we have you to thank for that."

"Look over there," Graf said, saving Paulie the embarrassment of coming up with a reply.

The gate was lifting and a small group of people carrying large backpacks came out. Two of them wore military uniforms, but the others were dressed in civilian clothes though they were, Paulie noticed, clean and in good condition.

"Foraging party," Paulie said. "Though surely this area must have been stripped clean by now?"

Lee shook his head. "Seattle's a big city and there are plenty of apartment blocks not far from here. It would take years to strip them of everything useful. I guess they send out their expeditionary force to seize people and supplies in large quantities, then use local scavenging to top up the stocks."

"I think we should follow them and get some answers. Just me and one other. Not you, *Pastor*. Jon?"

Graf looked uncertainly at her, but his answer was cut off by Tucker. "With respect, Sheriff, Jon here's a good cop, but what you need is a military man and that's me."

Paulie glanced across at Graf, who gave the tiniest of nods. She wasn't sure she felt comfortable trusting a man who'd come so close to disobeying her orders, but she'd appointed him as a deputy and if she wasn't going to trust him in situations like this, she should have removed him back in Arbroath when she'd had the chance.

"Okay. Get your stuff together. You two get the truck ready for a quick exit. If we're not back in three hours, get yourselves out of here under cover of dark."

"We're going nowhere without you," Graf said.

Paulie took his hand. "If we're not back in that time, Jon, then we're not coming back. But I'll be careful, honest. You know me."

Graff mumbled something noncommittal and then handed Tucker's pack to him. "Oh, and Marvin: I hold you personally responsible for making sure the sheriff gets back safely. Do you understand me?"

Tucker's eyes narrowed as he held Graff's stare but, after a moment, he nodded and followed Paulie out.

RAMOS AND TUCKER SHADOWED the foraging party as it headed into a residential area. They kept their weapons in their hands and followed as far behind the group as they could without the risk of losing them. Dusk was falling as they passed a big blue self-storage building and climbed a hill lined with single story houses.

The party was walking along the low picket fences without looking to the left or right—they knew exactly where they were going. As Paulie reached the first house, she glanced across to see that the door was open and two black bags lay outside, with cable ties sealing the top.

Marvin touched her arm and crouched down as their quarry stopped a few houses up. Each took a white boiler suit from their pack and climbed into it. Two of the suited figures went into the house and the rest dispersed, two by two, into the neighboring properties.

Paulie gestured right and Marvin followed her around the back of the first bungalow, the one that had been cleared on a previous expedition. They flitted into the garden, keeping low, until they were around the back of the house.

"Oh, my G—" Paulie moaned, before slapping her hand over her mouth.

The remains of a bonfire lay on the lawn. Blackened garden furniture and firewood piled around an upright post. And tied to the post were the charred remnants of what had once been a human being. The legs had been totally consumed, but the torso remained, and, at the top, the head was untouched by flames.

"Didn't happen long ago," Marvin whispered. "Couple of nights, I reckon."

The victim's face was twisted into a grimace of unimaginable agony, eyes staring at the heavens as if begging for deliverance. A young man, his shoulder length hair fell over the collar of a white boiler suit.

"Animals," Marvin said.

"Come on," Paulie responded, dragging her eyes from the hideous scene. "Let's get behind one of the houses without a guard." It was simple math—there were a dozen boiler suited house cleaners and two armed men watching them. That was the reason, presumably, for such brutal treatment of transgressions.

The guards were standing on either side of the road, each outside one house. She and Marvin slid until they had two properties between them and the guards. They wouldn't have long, but she needed answers. She had to understand what was going on here—she couldn't return to Arbroath without knowing the true nature of the threat to the north.

They found a side door. Paulie could hear heavy footsteps inside. The workers were dragging something across the floor. Her nose burned with the stench emerging through the gaps in the door frame. "I think they're disposing of a body," she said, gasping, "so we're going to have to wait for them."

Marvin's face dropped. "In there?" he hissed.

Paulie nodded and turned the door handle. It was locked, but Marvin levered open the small window above it, letting out a cloud of the disgusting gas, before reaching around and unlocking the door from the other side.

She pushed the door open gently, bracing herself against the smell, and they ran quickly through the living room, ignoring the black stain on the couch, and into the hallway, jumping into the shadows as the boiler suited workers came back in, wiping their gloves on their overalls.

At a nod from Paulie, they swept forward as the figures went to return to the living room. Marvin's knife caught the fading light as it swung into place over the jugular of the nearest worker, just as Paulie pressed her handgun against the forehead of the other.

"Silence!" she hissed. "Now, into the kitchen."

They followed the two figures inside and shut the door.

"Who are you?" the first stammered, as they were released.

"We're cops from out of town," Paulie said. "And we want some answers. Good grief, you're women."

The one who'd spoken first pulled her hood down. "Of course. This is women's work, or so we're told. But look, the guard will be here any minute and if they find you here..."

"Yes, we've seen what they do to those who cross them, but we can handle ourselves," Paulie said.

The other woman, of Latino appearance, shook her head vigorously. "No, you must not do that. If you kill the guards, we cannot return, and if we do not return, they will kill our friends. And they will find us."

"Then answer our questions quickly," Marvin rumbled, silencing the women.

"Tell us about the settlement. Who runs it and how did you come to be there?"

The women exchanged glances and the one who'd first spoken, a middle-aged woman with heavy bags under her glasses, responded. "It is run by Colonel Melua. He and his band came to our town and took everyone they could find, and all our possessions."

"Are you imprisoned?"

"Yes. We have converted some buildings to live in, though they are getting overcrowded, especially with the new ones who arrived today, poor things, I wish there was something we could do about them — "

Paulie cut off the woman's stream of consciousness. "Okay, I've got the picture. What are the people used for?"

"Some of the men are taken into the militia. Colonel Melua, he calls it his New Model Army, though they are really just *bandidos*," The Latino woman replied. "The rest he puts into work details or uses for menial tasks around the compound. He says we will move out soon, to somewhere better, but I do not know."

"So, you're held against your will?"

The first woman shrugged. "There are gates and razorwire, but where would I go if I escaped? I did not want to come here, but I would have died if I'd stayed where we were. This life is better than no life. But you must go!"

"Lydia, Maria, how are you getting on?"

Paulie cursed to herself and waved the two women out of the kitchen. She heard footsteps on the path before they echoed in the hallway.

"There you are. What have you been doing? There ain't time for chit chatting. Darn women. Now just you get on wi—What's that you say?"

"Don't kill him," whispered Paulie, though she wasn't sure Marvin heard her.

The door burst open, and a shot rang out. Paulie grabbed the arm and pulled it inside. Cries came from the road and a whistle blew in the gathering darkness. She brought her fist down on the man's head and he fell back, senseless.

"We'll split up," she said. "Meet back at the armory."

Marvin shook his head. "Nah, better chance together."

"That's an order. And if I don't make it, tell him Paulie says 'Wiggie' and he'll know you're not responsible. It was the name he gave his favorite dog as a child."

She sprang up. "You head out the back, I'll lead them off."

Marvin went to protest, but she'd run into the night.

PAULIE KEPT HERSELF VISIBLE for long enough to draw the remaining shooter behind her. If she killed the man, then the women would suffer and, even though she'd been betrayed by them, she didn't want that to happen. She was running in the opposite direction to the route back to the armory where the others were hiding.

She darted between two houses. Now it was time to lose her pursuer—Marvin should be half way back to the others by now. Graf would be furious. But Paulie wasn't going back. She'd never intended to.

Smith's suggestion of this fool's errand had presented the perfect opportunity. She was finally going to deal with the long-borne burden of her daughter's fate. One way or another, she would find out what had happened to Luna.

Paulina Ramos hid beneath a willow tree in the garden of what had once been a well-appointed dwelling and watched the guard run past. She waited for ten minutes and then headed from yard to yard. She was looking for a vehicle. Paulie was heading south.

Don't worry, darling. Mommy's coming.

Chapter 12

Solly

A SET OF STEPLADDERS had been placed beneath a street light, and Solly watched as Carl climbed them at gunpoint. It was now mid-morning on the day after Neil's murder and they'd just come from his graveside. As part of his punishment, Carl had been forced to dig the pit and fill it in, trembling in abject fear as he labored.

A noose hung from the light and a man Solly didn't recognize climbed the other side of the ladder and looped it around Carl's neck. He spoke a few words to the condemned man and descended.

Hanna stepped from the gathered crowd and stood beside the base of the light. As she opened her mouth, the man on the ladder began to cry.

"Please. Please. I'm beggin' you, Hanna," he sobbed. "I was wrong to do it, I know, but I just wanted their weapons to protect us. You know I've been faithful. Done my best by you."

A woman standing to Solly's right spoke. "He's right, Hanna. He saw off them bikers. He's kept us safe."

Hanna waited for a moment, perhaps to see if there would be any further protests. "If we are to survive as a community, then we must respect the rule of law and we must be true to our word. When we offer sanctuary, we must provide it. There are enough weapons on that truck to kill every one of us and if our visitors had suspected us of being faithless, then we would all be dead now."

"This man's attempt to steal these weapons would be cause enough to have him banished from the community but last night he killed someone who had sought our protection — "

"I didn't mean to," Carl wailed. "Honest to God, I swear I didn't mean to kill him."

Hanna turned to look up at him. "No, you meant to kill them all, Carl. And you were going to drive away in their truck and leave us to pick up the pieces. A life here obeying the rules got a bit stale, didn't it?"

"No! It weren't like that. I swear it. Please Hanna."

She faced the crowd again. "People of Breezewood, you granted me full executive powers when you elected me mayor and so I don't need your approval to punish this man. But I invite any here to speak for him if you will."

Carl's wide eyes scanned the faces of the people watching him, begging for someone to plead for him.

The woman who'd spoken before was the only taker. "Like I said, Hanna, he has fought for us. That ought to count for something."

Hanna nodded gravely. "You speak wisely, Christine."

She stepped to the side and gestured to the man standing beside the ladder. In one movement, he kicked it away and, with a shriek, Carl fell before, like the cracking of a whip, he jerked and kicked for a few moments and then was still.

Solly stood, open mouthed, at the hideous spectacle. The crowd gasped as one but went silent as Hanna put her hands up. "He has been put out of his misery, as a kindness, but let no one be in any doubt that if our community is to survive, it must be just. Without law, we have nothing but anarchy. We do not have the facilities to keep prisoners, so justice must be swift and, perhaps, harsh. But we can have no dead wood in Breezewood."

Ross, who'd been standing in Solly's shadow and under his instructions had not looked at the makeshift gallows or the man hanging from them, tugged on Solly's arm. "Can we go now?"

"Sure," he responded, and turned to leave these people to their grim business.

The people of Breezewood had filled the jerry cans with diesel and had added some of the food they'd gathered in their foraging. Solly pulled out the rifle and handed it to Hanna who was striding across the hotel parking lot.

"Thank you," she said. "You are welcome to stay longer, if you'd like. I'm truly sorry about your friend."

Solly lifted his pack into the cab. "We need to get back to the road, but thanks for the offer."

"Or perhaps you don't like our way of delivering justice?"

He turned back to her and shrugged. "I came pretty close to killing him myself last night. Neil had a family that survived the Long Fall, you know. A miracle. And he was a good man. Didn't deserve to die. Maybe his killer did."

"I'm sure you think I'm a hard woman, Solly, but the world needs people like me right now, otherwise we'd all be following low-lifes like Carl, the ones who shout loudest and wave their weapons around. The community is better off without him and his idiot accomplice."

She embraced him and wished them both a safe journey. "What about Ross? Do you not think he'd be safer here?"

"Why don't you ask him. He's man enough to make his own mind up."

Ross accepted her hug. "No thanks, ma'am. I'll stick with Solly. He'd be lost without me."

THEY HEADED OUT ONTO I-76 which soon became snarled up again and, in the end, Solly was forced onto the country roads that shadowed it. They were heading for Pittsburgh, aiming to pass it on the south side as Solly had no desire to head into the city. It seemed to him that however horrific the countryside might be, it would be an order of magnitude worse in the urban areas.

Every hour or two, they'd head back toward the highway to check whether it was passable and found that, between the cities, there were long stretches where, with care, they could pick their way between the rotting vehicles.

After their departure from Breezewood, they'd spoken together for a long time as both processed the loss of Neil. They'd known him for only a few days, but they realized, now he was gone, that he'd become a vital part of their little unit. He'd also been the prime source of motivation to get the accursed cylinder across country. Neil knew a lot more about it than Solly did and had been totally convinced that it needed to be delivered to someone in Arbroath. His story about Annabel Lee and the corporation she founded had helped fill in some of the background and Solly no longer doubted that their mission was critical, he just wished someone else had been burdened with it or, if not, that Neil were here to help. And to finish the story. So much was still unclear to him.

Ross had taken the loss of Neil even harder. The two had become close—though in a more brotherly way than Solly's relationship with him, which, although he didn't care to admit it, was more like father son. Once the dialog had quietened, Ross sat looking out the window as the wintry countryside passed and Solly could almost hear the wheels turning in his mind.

They'd reached the other side of Pittsburgh as the sky began to darken. Ross spotted a sign to Chippewa Golf Club, and they followed the long looping lane around to the parking lot in front of the red painted clubhouse. Surprisingly, it was still intact, and it was with some regret that Solly smashed the window and opened the door. There was a small bar inside, and they made themselves comfortable on the padded benches. Though they were in the middle of nowhere, after the events of the previous night, they decided to take two-hour stints on guard duty, though Solly left the boy to sleep for the final shift.

The following day dawned bright and crisp. It was a reluctant Solly who pulled his legs out of the sleeping bag and immediately into his cold jeans. Ross was snoring and Solly left him as he went in search of any food that might still be edible. To his delight he found a vending machine full of snacks in the golf shop, so it was with an arm full of chocolate and potato chips that he woke Ross up.

They joined I-70 just west of Bentleyville and made good progress that morning, though Solly's eyes had become heavy by 11 a.m. and they were forced to stop for lunch, so he could boil up some water for coffee. The roads here were less congested, but they were still forced to divert onto the grass roadside from time to time. They spent a frustrating and backbreaking hour pushing cars out of the way when they became trapped between two crash barriers, the worst of it was having to open the vehicles up to release their handbrakes. Solly took this upon himself and resolved to burn his clothes at the first opportunity.

The bright weather of the morning was replaced with dreary rain and dark clouds, and the hours passed as they felt like ants crawling across a desert getting nowhere fast. When they were approaching Wheeling, WV, they found themselves at the back of a nose-to-tail logjam. As a parting gift, Hanna had given them a road atlas to replace the torn out map sheets they'd been using and Ross found their location quickly enough.

"There's a tunnel up ahead," he said. "We're not gonna go through it are we?"

"No way. I'll get us off the interstate and we'll cut across country." The memory of their nightmare journey through that tunnel in New York was still fresh enough to put him off going anywhere near another.

They swung off to the south of the tunnel and took the bridge into the old town, passing wooden houses covered in flaking paint and rotten wood. A group of men ran out at them from the yard of one of those houses. Solly didn't stop to find out whether they were asking for help or attempting an ambush, he put his foot down and weaved the car expertly between the obstacles until they'd fallen behind.

They headed back onto the interstate and, over the hours that followed, saw a gradual increase in the number of vehicles on the road and the way became a little easier to find. They were heading for Columbus, but, again, intended to steer to the south of the city to avoid the urban area.

Their second night since leaving Breezewood was spent much less comfortably than the first. They'd passed nowhere that felt safe, so Solly resorted to pulling the car onto a side road within sight of the highway, then parking under a bridge. It was too cold to get out for any reason other than the natural essentials, so they sat in the cab, boiled up a can of soup and had it with some vacuum-packed pita bread he'd found in the golf restaurant that morning. Neither of them slept well, and it was with aching bones and a dull thumping headache that Solly started the car again in the morning.

By midday, they'd passed Columbus by. Solly had begun to recognize when they were nearing a major conurbation by the rising columns of smoke that gathered on the horizon each time. Columbus was no exception, and he wondered what was causing the fires. Presumably they were deliberately set, but they could have been either constructive or destructive. Maybe folks were just trying to keep warm.

They headed toward Springfield on a road that was becoming increasingly clear and so they reached the outskirts of Dayton, OH, shortly after another hurried and caffeine intensive lunch by the roadside. This time, the plan was to pass the city to the north and stay on the highway but, as they approached, they found the road blocked by a tanker on its side.

Luckily, there was a slip road just ahead of it, but Solly's guts tightened as they took it. An old Land Rover accelerated off the grass as they reached the bottom and headed toward them. Solly slammed his foot on the gas and the pickup lurched away, leaving the pursuers in its wake but, just as he thought they'd escaped, another car burst out from under a bridge and plowed into their side, throwing Ross across the seat.

Solly yanked on the steering wheel, desperately trying to bring the truck back under control as the tires squealed and he swerved back and forth in a desperate attempt to get away. Gunfire cracked from behind and he heard the metallic *dink, dink* of hits to the bodywork. They were catching up with him, and he steered randomly, hoping he could find his way back to the main road. *Dink, dink, dink.* The rounds seemed to be hitting the tailgate; it seemed they didn't want to damage whatever he had in the back.

Bingo, he was on an approach road back to I-70. But now, the pursuers were only a few car lengths back. His heart froze as there, blocking their approach to the highway, lay yet another car. Behind it the sun glinted on the barrels of the guns pointed in his direction.

"What are we going to do?" Ross said, his voice trembling.

"They've got us trapped. We've got to hope they'll settle for taking our stuff."

Solly said this to comfort the boy, but they didn't look like the kind who'd think twice about blowing their heads off.

He began slowing down as he approached the barrier and was just about to stop when there was a burst of fire—heavy, machine gun fire—from behind it and he saw, coming down from the highway, a Humvee. The makeshift barrier rocked as it was riddled with bullets, the bandits scattering far and wide as it approached. In his rearview mirror, Solly saw the car that had been chasing him do a handbrake turn and speed away in a cloud of burning rubber.

He couldn't follow them, or he'd be in their hands again. The Humvee looked legitimate and was being handled with practiced precision, but he had no idea whether they were genuine military or whether he'd just swapped one deadly situation for another.

He brought the car to a full halt as soldiers jumped down and crouched, carbines pointing at them. Someone in military uniform got down from the front and walked toward Solly's car. He and Ross got out, their empty hands held high as he approached.

"As I see it, you folks were being pursued by those scum," he said. "Call themselves The Wolverines, but they pretty soon high tail it away when they're outgunned. Have I got that right?"

Solly nodded vigorously, "Yes, we were just passing through and they ambushed us."

"Thought so. My name's Corporal Kuchinsky." He put out his hand and Solly shook it.

"Solly Masters. Who are you with?"

The man smiled. "Well, different military divisions don't mean squat anymore, but I was just a grunt. Got my stripe when the call went out and now I'm a part of the joint forces out of Wright-Patterson Air Force Base. We're trying to clean up a little and, lucky for you, you're on our patrol route today. I guess you boys would like somewhere to freshen up and set yourself right?"

"Thanks for the offer, but I think we'd rather get back on the road," Solly said, as his heart slowed to a more normal beat.

Again, the corporal smiled. "Sorry boys, but we're under standing orders to bring in anyone we find on the roads. It's one way we get intelligence about what's happening elsewhere."

As he spoke, he waved at the covering soldiers, and they jogged past him. "We'll just give your pick up the once over and then you can follow us back."

Solly flipped down the punctured tailgate and rolled back the cover before watching two of the soldiers searching through his stuff.

"What's this?" Kuchinsky said.

Solly's heart sank. "It's just a safe with valuables in. Personal stuff."

"I'm afraid I'm gonna have to ask you to open it."

"Sorry, I can't do that," Solly said miserably.

The corporal shook his head sadly. "In that case, we'll be forced to destroy it. Can't risk taking anything unknown into the base. Hand me a grenade," he said to one of the others.

"I'll do it," Solly muttered, and he leaned forward to key the combination. "But please don't get it out."

Too late. The corporal had reached inside and pulled out the cylinder.

"What is it? It looks a bit like an artillery round, but I don't reckon it's a weapon."

"It's mine," Solly said. "It's of no military value. Please return it and let us go."

"Sorry, Mr. Masters, but we're taking this and you're going to follow us back to the base. We'll get some of our eggheads to take a look at it and see what we can find out if you won't spill the beans."

Solly got back into the truck and watched as the Humvee turned around. The cylinder and the hopes of the human race were now in the hands of what was left of the military.

Chapter 13

Solly felt like a country bumpkin on his first trip into the city when he entered the mess hall at the Wright-Patterson Air Force Base. Not since the Long Fall had he seen so many people together in one place. Civilians occupied just over half the area, generating a hubbub of chatter and laughter that reminded Solly of a shopping mall on Christmas Eve.

Solly and Ross sat in the military zone next to their escort, Corporal Kuchinsky. A likable man who was full of energy, Kuchinsky was, nonetheless, their roving jailer, keeping tabs on them until their inevitable meeting with the base commander.

Looking around at the milling people, the running children and the general vivacity of the place, Solly couldn't help but feel a surge of hope for the future. But then, what of the cylinder? If Neil was to be believed—and Solly didn't doubt him—a second wave was coming that would, at the very least, see to the enslavement of these people. More likely, according to Neil, it would lead to their deaths.

But if it was a weapon of some sort, then surely the military were the right people to have it. This place seemed to be the real deal, not the camp of some bandit with stolen equipment. According to Kuchinsky, the call had been put out far and wide for surviving military personnel to gather here and to bring civilians with them if they wished to come.

The base was too vast to protect, so one corner had been carved out, protected on three sides by the original razor wire, chain link and checkpoints, and on the other by a recently constructed wire fence made from pieces cut from the perimeter. It was, perhaps, a fourth of its original area, but the safe zone included all the principal buildings and facilities, so it was large enough to house the hundreds of people gathered here.

Judging by their variety, the new residents weren't families, but rather groups of individuals gathered together with the common purpose of seeking safety and shelter behind the shield of the military.

Solly learned that the base generated its own electricity, with scavenging parties such as Kuchinsky's sent out to locate and drain the local gas stations, and had its own water towers. Food was scavenged from distribution centers, often at the cost of a firefight with the bandits protecting it. It was an efficient operation and, at the center of it, like a spider pulling on the threads, was its commander.

COLONEL GEORGE MCBRIDE WAS an impressive man. Stocky, tanned and with close cropped black hair pebble dashed with gray, he stood to greet Solly and Ross as they entered his office. A perfectly pressed blue uniform complete with silver wings and a chest full of ribbon completed the impression of the consummate professional soldier.

"Mr. Masters, thank you for joining me," he said in a voice that was rich and deep. "I trust Corporal Kuchinsky ensured you were fed and watered."

Solly took his hand but couldn't compete with the firm grip. "He did, thank you. We're much refreshed."

"And keen to be on your way? Or would you prefer to remain for a while and help us secure this community?"

Ross and Solly took seats in front of the Colonel's desk as he sat down. "We'd like to move on, though we'd appreciate a place to stay for tonight."

"Of course. Where will you go?"

"That depends on you," Solly said, carefully considering what he was going to say. "If you will return the device I was carrying, then I'll continue west. If not, I'll return to Hagerstown."

McBride seemed to consider this as he leaned back in his chair. "What do you know of this device?"

This was the crunch. Two opposing forces wrestled for control of Solly's mind. On the one hand, Neil had insisted that the cylinder had to be delivered into the right hands and he had never suggested that this might include giving it to the military, official or otherwise. On the other hand, he couldn't deny it would be wonderful to simply give it to this impressive man and drive back to the farmhouse before heading south to Texas. He imagined the weight of another two thousand miles on the road west being lifted from his shoulders and almost buckled. Almost.

"I don't know a lot," he responded. "But let me ask you, what do you think caused the long fall?"

"The long fall? Is that what you call it? To us it's the Massacre. Do you know, out of the personnel on this base only two in a hundred survived that night? I watched hundreds of the men and women under my command fall down dead as if they'd been gassed. It became obvious quickly that the civilian population hadn't been hit quite so hard, but still, it was carnage."

He regarded Solly for a moment before continuing. "As for causes, my scientists tell me they think it's related to a Bones malfunction. They think it's possible the BonesWare system was hacked, and a virus injected."

"Hacking BonesWare is considered impossible," Solly responded. "It would have been a lot easier for the manufacturer to insert malicious code, after all."

McBride leaned forward, all attention now. "Are you suggesting the Lee Corporation deliberately killed 95% of their customers? Why would they do something like that? "

"I don't know the detail. All I do know is that they build and license BonesWare, so every implant runs their code. The device I had in my car is also built by them, but it has a role to play in stopping a second wave."

"Explain yourself," McBride said.

Solly sighed. "Again, I don't know much. I was given the device by a rogue agent within Lee Corp—which is still a functioning unit—and told to take it out of New York. I believe it's something they consider extremely valuable. I was then tracked down by two other agents and they persuaded me to take it to a town in Washington State where it could be handed over to someone who knows what to do with it."

As he said this out loud, Solly realized how hazy his understanding was and how much he'd been prepared to do based on little more than hints and gut feeling.

"So, it's a weapon," McBride said.

"I honestly don't know. I don't think so, not in the traditional sense of an explosive device. But it is fitted with some sort of transponder, so it needs shielding, that's why it was in the safe."

McBride nodded and stood up. "I'll let our technicians know. Thank you, Mr. Masters, but I believe this device is safest here. I will have you assigned some temporary quarters and will be pleased to refuel your vehicle and provide supplies for your return journey."

There was no point in arguing. The colonel had the power to do what he wished with Solly, Ross and the cylinder and, after all, if it was taken from him by the military then he could hardly be blamed. And he wouldn't have to drive across the country. He saw their faces: Janice, Bella, Jake and Maddie, and quietly made his exit.

Solly was jerked awake by the sound of an explosion followed by the *rat-at-at* of small arms fire. He flicked the light on as Ross sat up in the bed next to his.

"What is it?" Ross murmured.

Solly thrust his legs into his pants. "The Lees," he said. "Coming for the cylinder."

"They'd attack a base?"

Ross was right to be doubtful. So far, all they'd seen of the Lee Corp security forces was the squad that came to retrieve Khaled in New York City and the two who'd killed Jeremiah. However, it could hardly be a coincidence that, on the day he'd brought the cylinder here, the base came under attack.

"You stay here," Solly called.

"No!"

He turned and grabbed the boy by the arms. "Look, I'm going to try to get to the cylinder before they do, and I don't need to have you to worry about as well as myself." He drew Ross into a hug, then ruffled his hair. "I'll be back."

"Alright, Arnie," Ross said, though his face betrayed his terror.

"If anything happens to me, stay here where it's safe. Get word to the farmhouse—maybe they can come here too."

They had been found lodging in a civilian block and the flashes of gunfire were coming from an area to their south. Solly collided with a man who emerged from another room.

"Where's the science block?"

"Never heard of it. There's the tech lab, though, but it's down there." He waved a hand in the direction of the gunfire. "Building C5."

Solly ran out into the darkness, moving from one puddle of light to the next and, all the time, looking out for figures in black uniforms. He was passed by squads of soldiers and was ordered back to the civilian area more than once, but he waited for them to head away and then followed them in the direction of the main complex of buildings.

Beyond, on the airstrip outside the safe zone, sat three helicopters, the flashes of gunfire reflecting from their glossy black exteriors. Solly reached a building and looked up at the plate. D3.

Gunfire from his right and he dodged sideways into the gap between buildings and crouched down. So far, everyone he'd seen with a gun was wearing a variant of the standard US military uniform and was heading toward the command center.

He ran down the side of the low white painted brick building, ducking below the windows, until he reached the corner and peered around it. He could see figures running in the distance, so he headed to the left, away from them, in the hope that there'd be some logic to the numbers and that he was now in row C.

Darting across the gap between rows, he heard someone order him to stop and then, almost immediately, rounds spat past him, one shattering a window in the building he was heading toward. Just as quickly as it started, however, the gunfire stopped as his attackers turned their attention to the main battle area.

Building C3. He crouched and ran along it as quickly as his ungainly posture allowed. C4. He was now heading toward the sounds of fighting, and he prayed that they hadn't gotten there first.

This was it. He turned ninety degrees, expecting at any moment for someone to call out or simply shoot him without warning. A plate beside the door said *Technical Lab*, and he took a deep breath before turning the handle and plunging inside.

"Halt, or I fire," a voice called. Solly stopped instantly and put his hands up. The building was made up of a single main room and there, at a bench half way down, stood a man pointing a handgun at him, its tip trembling.

"It's alright," Solly responded, forcing down his fear. "I'm not with the Lee Corporation—they're the ones attacking the base. Have you got the cylinder here?"

"You can't have it! It's too dangerous."

Solly edged forward. "Look, I'm not armed. Can I come closer?"

The man didn't respond, so Solly moved toward the bench. On it sat something cylindrical, but it didn't look like the device Solly had carried.

"Yes, this is it. I covered it in shielding as the commander said it could be tracked."

"I guess you added the shielding elsewhere and then brought the device here?"

The technician looked surprised. "How could you know that?"

"Because the Lees have pinpointed their attack on the last known location and if you'd done it here, they'd have broken down the door and taken it by now. My name is Solly, by the way."

"Brendon."

Solly felt sorry for the man. Barely out of his twenties, he was at the center of something much, much larger than he was and way beyond his resources. Felt familiar.

"We can't let the Lee Corporation get their hands on this, Brendon, and the only way to stop that is to get it away from the base. Do you understand that?"

Brendon shook his head uncertainly. "I've had barely enough time to do any analysis. I'm not sure what it is, let alone what it does."

"Neither am I, but people I trust have told me it's vital to stopping the Lee Corporation from unleashing a second wave that will kill or enslave the survivors of the Long Fall."

The shaking became more pronounced. "I hardly understand a word of what you just said."

Solly came right up to the bench as Brendon put down the gun, looking for all the world like a lost child. "I don't have time for a full explanation, not that I have one, to be honest. I'm as certain as I can be that they were behind the killings, acting through the BonesWare—"

"Yes! That's my theory. Mine was offline that day. It's not a perfect theory, though, because there are many among the survivors with working BonesWare implants—"

"That's right. But I think they plan to unleash a second wave to mop up survivors."

Brendon threw his hands up in astonishment. "But why would they do that? That's insane!"

Solly shrugged. "I don't know, I honestly don't. My contact said they intend the second wave to enslave rather than kill, but he also said they were wrong, and it would lead to another massacre. Extinction, Brendon, that's what we're fighting here."

While he was speaking, Solly's ears strained for any sign that the fighting was getting closer. There was no time.

With a speed that surprised even him, he reached out and grabbed the gun before turning it on Brendon, who shrieked in fear.

"I'm sorry, I just don't have time to debate this. It needs to get away and I'm going to take it. I don't want to have to shoot you, I really don't. But if I have to, I will."

"Take it, take it!" Brendon said. He reached down and disconnected the cylinder from the diagnostic equipment and held it out to Solly at arm's length, as if it might infect him or even explode.

Solly took it from him. "I wish you well, Brendon. Keep yourself safe." He turned and ran back to the door before pulling it open.

"Solly," Brendon called from behind the bench. "One thing I did find out."

"What is it? Hurry!"

"There's a mind inside that thing," he called, his voice wavering. "It's alive."

Chapter 14

Bella

Jake's recovery had been borderline miraculous. It had been only three days since they'd arrived at Lackland Air Force Base, and most of that first day had been spent waiting to be processed.

Once Jake's condition had been assessed he was rushed to the base's infirmary and operated on within the hour. As expected, he'd signed his enlistment papers before being admitted and so, as he was now under the care of the military, Bella had been forced to wait in temporary accommodation until the news that the operation had been successful finally arrived.

She and Maddie had been allowed to visit him at his bedside over the following couple of days and by the evening of the day after their arrival, he was walking confidently on his bandaged leg.

"Look at this, Mom," he said before opening the locker beside his bed and pulling out military fatigues. He held up the jacket. "My name will go there: Private Jacob Masters. How cool is that?"

Bella forced a smile. "You know you'll have to follow orders, don't you? You won't be able to argue with every single decision like at home?"

"Mom, I'm in the military, of course I'll have to follow orders," he said, before sitting on his bed. "I've already started my training."

Jake handed over a small black device with a row of buttons and the words Basic Orientation on a paper label. "It's like an MP3 player. I've been told I have to work through the whole thing, then I'll be tested, and if I pass, I'll get to join my new unit for basic training."

"That's nice, dear."

"I didn't know Texas had been independent before, did you?"

"Yes, dear. But then I paid a little more attention at school."

Jake deflated a little, but then puffed out his chest again. "Well, whatever. I'm gonna help it be independent again."

"And New Mexico and Louisiana," Maddie piped up.

Jake shrugged. "I suppose so. My training only talks about Texas. Maybe in the other states they have their own training."

"What have you learned about the new president?"

"Oh, loads," Jake said. "He's a veteran, you know. Fought in Iraq and Afghanistan. Purple heart. Lots of other military awards. He saw what was going on after the Long Fall and decided to do something about it. He's a great man."

Bella's heart sank at hearing him talk like this. In general, as with most teenagers, Jake wasn't impressed by anyone over the age of twenty-five, but this had all the hallmarks of an obsession. Maybe even brainwashing.

"Well, I hope he looks after you. That's all that matters to me," Bella said, as she sat alongside her son and put her arms around his shoulders. Will this be the last time I do this? she thought, then, pulling herself together, she looked up at the clock. "Visiting time's over. We'll come in and see you again tomorrow."

Jake smiled. "Good. I don't think I'll be here much longer, though. The doc reckons I'll be ready to go join my team in a day or two."

BELLA AND MADDIE HARDLY exchanged a word as they walked back to the accommodation block where they shared a room. The base was a bustling hive of humanity and it had taken them a couple of days to get used to the crowds and the sheer level of activity. The place felt like an ants' nest preparing to make war on a neighbor.

They picked up a coffee each and took it back to their room. It was an adapted office block as the barracks were all being used by the military. Families of incoming recruits waited here to be assigned permanent quarters, and Bella wondered whether she and Maddie were going to be trapped in this new state or whether they'd be allowed out again. She'd been forced to reconcile herself to the fact that Jake was, for now, in the military, but she had no desire to stay here long term.

For one thing, the rules and regulations of the TLX were harsh and authoritarian. She'd seen no evidence of any civilian involvement in the new government, so all laws were passed in the interests of the military alone. Justice was fast and brutal, though this had only become apparent once they'd arrived at the base. The countryside outside Lackland was, to all appearances, at peace, but almost the first thing they'd seen when they arrived on the base was a group of prisoners in orange boiler suits being marched somewhere. They'd since discovered that, behind the makeshift prison block, there stood a set of gallows.

She wasn't completely naive. She knew well enough that strong government was needed in extraordinary times like these, but it was a thin line and, from what she'd seen, the TLX was stepping across it.

"Mom, what's this?"

Maddie had picked up an envelope that had been slid under the door of their room.

Bella ripped open the seal and read the letter inside. At the top was printed what she'd come to recognize as the symbol of the TLX.

To: Mrs. Isabella Masters 1029BH192

Miss Madeline Masters 1029BH193

You are hereby instructed to vacate your temporary accommodation and to report to the following locations to receive your work assignments.

Mrs. I Masters: Community Farm 14, reporting to Angelique Leguard

Miss M Masters: Cedar Ranch, reporting to James Ham

Full details follow.

"They're splitting us up?" Maddie said, her face white.

Bella was already pulling her coat around her shoulders and heading for the door.

MINUTES LATER, SHE WALKED up to the front desk of the administration building and slammed down her letter.

"Who do I see about this?" she snapped.

The uniformed young woman on the other side of the desk read the letter and shook her head. "You don't like your assignments?"

"I don't like the fact that my daughter and I are being split up!"

"It's standard policy."

"To separate families?"

The young woman leaned forward and lowered her voice. "No, to assign different duties to women of child bearing age."

For a moment, Bella was so shocked she couldn't speak. "And which of us does this apply to?"

"Your daughter."

"She's fourteen!" Bella hissed.

The woman nodded. "I understand this is a shock, but these are challenging times and it's government policy to ensure that the birth rate rises quickly to ensure the future." It was as if she was reading from a script.

"You mean she's going to be married off!"

"She has been found a suitable match."

"She's fourteen!!"

With a little shrug, the woman on the desk said, "It's always been legal to marry at that age in Texas."

After another momentary pause as Bella tried desperately to lubricate the gears of her mind, she grabbed the letter and pulled Maddie behind her out of the office.

"We're getting out of here," she whispered.

It took only minutes to get their belongings into the car, and only a few more for Bella and Maddie to rush to Jake's bedside and explain their departure. He was as shocked as they were at the prospect of Maddie being married off to a stranger, though it didn't obviously dent his resolve to serve in the military.

Bella wiped the tears of parting from her eyes as she sat behind the wheel. She'd told Jake that they were heading back to the beach house since it, for now, remained outside the control zone of the authorities. He was signed up for a year and, though even that seemed like an eternity, she doubted the authorities would let him out after so short a time. She was resigned, for now, to not seeing her son for the foreseeable future and so she sobbed as she turned the key. She had done her best to help him, but it was now her daughter she needed to think about

She remembered the words of Margaret, the little girl Ethan had introduced as his daughter. They were a fake family, but whereas Bella had assumed that Margaret had been adopted for her own sake, it now seemed likely that Ethan's wife had also been a stranger to him only weeks before. That wasn't going to be Maddie's future if Bella had any say in the matter.

The car pulled forward and Bella headed for the gate they'd entered through. The barrier was down, and a soldier came out of the guard box and walked toward her as she wound down her window.

"Yes ma'am?"

"I'd like to leave the base," Bella said, doing her best to keep her voice steady.

"Can I see your permit, ma'am?"

"Why would I need a permit to leave?"

The soldier removed his sunglasses and regarded her steadily. "Those are the regulations, ma'am. Movement into or out of the base is controlled by permit. No permit, no exit."

Bella sagged. "Where do I get a permit?" she said, resignedly.

"The administration building," he responded. "Do you need directions?"

"No," Bella said. There was no escape this way, and likely no escape at all—Lackland was, after all, a military base.

She turned the car around as the tears started again.

They found two uniformed men in their room when they returned to it.

"Mrs. Masters," the first said, a tall man with a crisply ironed jacket of yellow and green camouflage. "Please explain your attempt to leave the base."

"Are we prisoners here?" Bella snapped.

"You are citizens of the free states of Texas, Louisiana and New Mexico. As such, you have a duty to obey orders."

Bella threw her arms up in frustration. "What orders?"

"I understand you received your orders in the form of a memo this morning."

"They weren't orders, they were accommodation assignments."

The man nodded. "Exactly. You were instructed to prepare to depart tomorrow, were you not?"

"Yes, but I assumed that was only if we wanted to take up the offer."

"I understand. What you saw as an offer was, in fact, an order. I am pleased to clear up the confusion. You will take up your assignments."

"So, this is a police state now, is it? This wonderful new start for humanity? Where are we, North Korea?"

The officer's face tightened. "Not a police state, no. The people of the TLX are under military protection at present, though that is intended to be temporary. In the meantime, citizens who seek our protection and help are expected to do their duty and follow lawful orders."

"My son is doing his duty," Bella spat.

"And so must you," the man said, before turning to Maddie. "Miss Masters, please come with me. I think it best that you begin your assignment immediately."

"Mom!" Maddie cried, grabbing Bella's arm.

"You can't do this!" Bella said. "Please, don't take her away! She's all I have left."

"We have all lost, Mrs. Masters, and we must all make sacrifices as we build a new country for children. Your daughter will help with that."

He turned to the man behind him and gave a gesture.

The man, who wore sergeant's stripes on his arm, stepped forward, his face grim and held out a hand to Maddie. "Miss," he said.

"Don't let them, Mom!" Maddie cried, wrapping herself around Bella.

The sergeant took hold of her and gently, though remorselessly, pulled her away.

"Mom!!"

Bella threw herself at the sergeant, wrapping her arms around his thick neck and pulling him backwards. For a moment, he staggered as, with a shriek, Maddie was taken from his arms by the officer.

The sergeant brought his elbow around and caught Bella on the ribs. She cried out in pain, tears filling her eyes, as she fell to the floor. She scrambled onto her knees to see that they were already opening the door, dragging Maddie, who was kicking and yelling, through.

Bella howled at them to stop, but last thing she saw of her daughter was Maddie's red, desperate face as tears streamed down her cheeks. She screamed as she was bundled out and Bella sobbed until she felt as though she was an empty, soulless, husk. Father, son and daughter lost over the course of three days. Her world was now truly ended. She had no one.

There was the click of a key turning in a lock.

She spent hours there, lost in despair until her door was unlocked again and, feeling as though she needed to do something, anything, she went in search of Jake. She didn't know what she expected him to be able to do about it but was told he'd already been moved to quarters elsewhere on the base from where he'd join his new unit. Her mood, briefly galvanized by the thoughts of seeing her son, fell lower than ever and she shuffled back toward the civilian quarters without noticing where she was or what she was doing.

"The line's moving, lady," a gruff voice said from behind her.

Bella found herself in the canteen queue, a long gap in front of her. She moved forward, wondering how she'd gotten here and then realized how hungry she was. Clearly her subconscious had brought her here while her thinking mind was wallowing in despair.

She ran her tray along the counter, nodding and shaking her head as she went, then took it to the least occupied table she could find.

Bella sat down and absentmindedly picked her way through her meal, thinking of nothing, seeing nothing.

"Bella, thank the Lord."

She recognized the voice and something about its urgent tone cut through her malaise. Raising her eyes, she looked into a familiar face. A face she thought she'd never see again.

"Nathan?"

"You remember me, then?" he said, sitting down opposite her. A smile spread across the handsome face of Nathan Woods.

"I thought you were dead?"

The smile turned into a grim chuckle. "Why would you think that?"

"The house was burned down."

"Yes, I'm sorry about that. I wasn't inside."

She noticed the subtle emphasis on the noun, and she suspected that Nathan had lured the remaining bikers into the house and set it alight with them trapped inside. Right now, however, this didn't concern her. "What are you doing here?"

The smile disappeared. "I was hiking toward Houston when I ran into someone who told me of the new government in Texas, so I made my way in this direction. I've been here for a few weeks, even got my stripes." He turned his arm to show two chevrons. "Sergeant Woods."

Bella tried to smile but found it impossible. "They took Maddie, Nathan."

"I know. I'm sorry."

"And Jake's been enlisted."

Nathan nodded. "I know that, too. I asked to have him assigned to my unit so I can keep an eye on him."

Suddenly, Bella felt as though at least some of the weight had been lifted from her shoulders. "Thank you, Nathan. Thank you so much."

She remembered the serious doubts she'd had about Woods when he'd executed a man in a parking lot, but right now she was relieved to know that he would watch out for her son.

"There's only so much I can do," he said. "But what I can do, I will."

Bella took his hands and squeezed them.

"Look, I can't help Maddie, but I can do something for you," he said, looking from left to right as if afraid of being overheard.

He reached into his pocket and slid a square laminated card across the table under his hand, pressing it into hers. "Don't look at it here."

"What is it?"

"A civilian pass," he said, barely moving his lips.

"Where did you get it?"

He shook his head slightly. "Never you mind. Just hand it in at the gate and they should let you through. If you take my advice, you'll go just before noon—there'll be a queue at that time and the guards don't check as thoroughly. Amateurs. There aren't many regulars like me in this new army."

"But where do I go?"

"Out of TLX. Take the back roads when you reach the border, they're not all barricaded. Jake told me about his grandfather—I suggest you find out what happened to him. Then go home. I'll do my best to find out about Maddie, though I can't do much for her."

Bella leaned forward. "I can't leave my children!"

"They need to know you're safe, Bella. It'll give them hope. It won't always be like this here," he said, though he sounded distinctly unsure.

She wiped her eyes. Jake was lost to her but being watched by a man who'd proven himself by saving their lives back at the old house. It was Maddie her heart ached for.

"Look, I know what you're thinking, but I reckon she's safe for a while."

"Safe from what?"

His face dropped. "You know. She won't be married until they've run tests to check her fertility. And, anyway, it makes sense to wait for her to grow a little before she becomes pregnant."

"She's not a sow," Bella hissed. The people at the next table turned to look at them, but she pulled herself together and squeezed Nathan's hand, making it look as though it was a simple lover's quarrel.

"I know, I'm just trying to reassure you a little."

Bella sat silently looking at the stern face of the young man. She drew in a deep breath. "Thank you, Nathan. I owe you more than I could ever repay."

"You saved my life," was the simple reply.

"My father did that. I wouldn't have stopped if he hadn't made me," she said, remembering the sight of the soldier as he lay in the road on that first night, looking like all the other dead bodies.

"Then go save your father," Nathan said.

Chapter 15

Paulie

Paulie awoke suddenly from a nightmare and let out a shriek of fear as her eyes opened onto utter blackness. It took several seconds for her to remember where she was and for her conscious mind to banish the monsters circling in her dreams.

She'd been driving south for two days, car hopping as each ran out of gas. Paulie couldn't even remember what make of vehicle she was sleeping in, but she knew it was at least the third different one. As dusk had fallen, she'd pulled into a service area beside I-5 at a place whose name she'd also forgotten. The gas station had been burned to the ground, but behind it lay a small group of industrial units. She'd driven the car into an empty one and pulled down the shutter behind her. She didn't want to think about what was causing the stink in here, but it was too late to go anywhere else, so she shut the windows and hunkered down.

With no one to share guard duty, she was forced to find the most deserted places to snatch a few hours of sleep when exhaustion forced her to rest. The journey so far had been a frustrating mix of picking her way between rotting vehicles, short stretches where she could put her foot down a little, and complete blockages that left her scrambling along the grass roadside or resorting to back roads.

One surprise was that, as she headed south, she began to notice people on the roads going north. Some were driving like her, others were walking. To begin with, they'd been traveling in small groups of two or three, but more recently the groups had gotten larger. She wondered where they were going but didn't stop. Paulie was on a mission to track down her daughter and, if she was still alive, to bring her to Arbroath and some semblance of safety.

What was that sound?

She sat up straight and drew her gun. Had she imagined it? Was it just the random noises a car's suspension makes when you move?

There it was again. A whimpering, pathetic moan. She pulled the flashlight out of the glovebox and shone it out of the grimy car windows but could see nothing. Icy fear laced her body but there was nothing else for it, she'd have to get out of the car and trace the source of the noise.

She opened the door of the car as quietly as she could and swung the torch light around the floor of the workshop, catching her breath on the ghastly smell. The beam illuminated metal racking stacked with dusty boxes full of car parts, but there was no sign of whatever was in here with her.

Paulie noticed she was holding her breath and made a conscious decision to draw in a deep gulp of the fetid air before edging around the car and checking the other side of the workshop. More shelving, more boxes and a trade counter near the side door.

The noise, and the worst of the smell, was coming from that direction. Moving slowly forward with her flashlight in one hand, her handgun in the other, she rounded the counter and swung the light around.

Green eyes flashed in the darkness, and she gave a yell, stepped back, drew a breath and looked again.

"Oh, you poor thing," she said, kneeling.

The dog was so thin that Paulie could count its ribs as she examined it with the beam of her flashlight. It looked up at her, making a mute appeal—but whether that should be deliverance from its suffering or a chance at salvation, Paulie couldn't guess. Was it beyond saving?

She stood up and the dog's eyes followed her as she walked back around the counter, its plaintive cry echoing in the dark workshop. Paulie had managed to scrounge some supplies on her journey and had hit it lucky with the car before this one which had a trunk full of food. She'd wondered at the time why its occupants had abandoned it, but that mystery was forgotten as she rummaged for the sterilized milk she knew was there. She had no idea whether this would be good for the dog, but it would at least show whether it had any life left in it. If it had no appetite, it was a lost cause.

When she returned, the dog had dragged itself a few inches out of its bed, but its back legs couldn't hold its weight. She found a bowl on one of the metal shelves, poured a little milk into it and put it down in front of the dog. With obvious and instant relish, the creature lapped it down in seconds. Well, that answered the first question. Since it was showing signs of life, she had an obligation to help it. And, besides, she liked the idea of having some company.

She sat, stroking the dog and comforting it as it drank the milk, and they then shared a can of meat. And, together, they waited for the night to end.

The dog, it turned out, was called Dany. As Paulie read the tag, it made her unaccountably sad to connect, for a moment, with the *Game of Thrones* fan who had once run this little workshop. She had no idea where the owner might be, but it was certain he or she was dead. Dany was a mongrel whose ancestry seemed to include elements of Golden Retriever and German Shepherd. She was mainly tan colored, with dark markings on her face and pointed ears, and she'd rallied quickly as soon as she'd been fed. There was no way of knowing how old she was until she'd fattened up a little, but Paulie guessed she was on the younger side.

Paulie found her lead, bowls and a supply of dry food in the little kitchenette at the back of the workshop. As she was packing them into the trunk, she turned to see Dany emerge from behind the counter. Her back legs were still very wobbly, and she was still emaciated, but a little food and water had worked wonders.

"Don't worry," Paulie said, "I wasn't going to leave you behind."

She put the harness around the dog's chest, and tightened it to fit, then used the lead to help haul her up onto the passenger seat, before opening the shutters and flooding the little unit with morning light. Fortunately, the smell in the workshop hadn't come directly from the dog, but rather from what she'd left behind, so she didn't need a bath.

TODAY'S MISSION WAS TO get past Portland. It was around a hundred miles south of where she'd stayed the night, so she'd decided to set off as soon as the sun was up. To her delight, she discovered some jerrycans out back containing gasoline, so she loaded those into the back of the SUV and, with Dany as her navigator, headed back onto I-5.

Within minutes, the dog was asleep on the front seat, so Paulie weaved in and out of the parked traffic without canine assistance, enjoying Dany's rhythmic snoring. She pulled over after a couple of hours and let the dog out for a comfort break. Dany's back legs were getting stronger, and she wolfed down the small portion of tinned meat Paulie gave her, licking the bowl with such fervor that it was all Paulie could do to deny her any more. Little and often, that made the most sense.

They got back in the car and made better progress. Dany stayed awake this time, enjoying the warmth of the heated car seat and air conditioning, and it was her barking that first alerted Paulie to movement. They were on a raised section of highway heading over a town and there was a collection of flat roofed buildings gathered around a series of fields to their right. Paulie could see what Dany had spotted—people were moving, lots of people.

She stopped the car and got out to take a look. She watched for ten minutes or so, looking for any sign of military equipment, but it looked for all the world like a peaceful settlement. Someone was cooking because white smoke rose from several points and she could just discern a deliciously rich aroma on the breeze. Dany could smell it too, Paulie could see her sticking her nose out of the open window of the car.

In the days that followed, Paulie couldn't explain what had prompted her to take the car off the highway and investigate this community. Perhaps it was fate at work.

A man carrying a shotgun stepped forward as she approached the makeshift barrier at the end of the approach road.

Dany started barking the instant she saw him but quieted at a command.

"Welcome to the showground," he said. Then he spotted Paulie's uniform. "Good grief, are you police?"

"My name's Sheriff Paulina Ramos," she said, flashing her badge at the wide-eyed guard. "I'm heading south and just wanted to stop by and see what you folks are up to."

The guard was a young man who looked as though he'd just wandered in from gathering the harvest. "Wow. Johnson's sure gonna be pleased to see you. Head right on in and I'll send a message. But you don't wanna be headin' south, that's where the worst of it is. Everyone's comin' this way."

Paulie wanted to ask more, but he'd withdrawn his head and was waving her past the barrier as it was lifted out of the way. She could hear him talking excitedly to the others there and watching her as she went.

A few people turned to glance at her as she drove into the car park of what looked like a convention center, but the general lack of interest suggested that arrivals were pretty commonplace. She locked the car, checked that her Glock was in its holster beneath her jacket and helped Dany out. The dog seemed delighted to be among people again, even managing to wag her tail as she made her unsteady way beside Paulie.

Paulie rubbed her hands against the chill and headed toward one of the many oil drum fires burning in the plaza outside the main building. A man and a woman stood beside the one she chose and returned her greeting cheerfully. When they told her they'd come from just north of LA, her heart froze for a moment, and she wondered why she was wasting her time here when she could be on the road south to find her daughter. She was just turning around when a voice called out to her.

"Sheriff!"

A large man was carving his way through the crowd, waving to her as he went. He approached with his hand out, almost crushing hers as she shook it.

"Johnson Green, mayor of this little community of Clark County," he said, his double chins wobbling in his enthusiasm.

"Paulina Ramos, sheriff of Arbroath," she said.

His expression froze mid wobble. "Arbroath? You're from there?"

"Yes," Paulie responded, surprised and mildly alarmed by his recognizing the name. "Do you know it?"

"I've never been there, but I've heard tell that it's a safe place. Surely, you've passed people walking north? That's where they're heading. We have so little room here."

The cogs of Paulie's mind ground as she considered this. "What do they imagine they'll find? It's hardly a nirvana."

"They're looking for safety, sheriff. But please let me give you a tour of our little community."

Reeling from this new problem for her hometown, she allowed herself to be guided toward the main building, Dany walking along beside her.

"We would certainly appreciate any advice you have for tightening up security," Green was saying as they walked through the double doors and inside.

"You have a generator," Paulie said, stating the obvious. One in three of the striplights were on, giving a dim but usable illumination to the white and beige interior of the building.

"Yes, finding enough fuel is one of our biggest challenges, so we only allow minimal lighting. People have to be sheltered, but we need light to work by."

They passed a public cafeteria in which small groups of people sat at tables looking out over the fields.

"My biggest concern is keeping the hospital supplied," Green said. "We're blessed to have two qualified doctors and half a dozen nurses but finding the drugs they need to do their job is a constant struggle."

The last thing Paulie wanted to do right now was look at sick people for fear of acquiring another chain of responsibility that would keep her from traveling south, but she had no choice as Green guided her gently but firmly in that direction. She tied up Dany outside and glanced back to see the dog watching her intently.

The lights were brighter here, and the hospital had the air of an efficiently organized operation as people moved with confidence from bed to bed.

"There's a hotel next door," Green said. "We got the beds from there."

There were perhaps a dozen patients in the little hospital, arranged around the wall facing inwards, hidden in the shadows from the light flooding through the windows. A woman in a white coat was examining a patient and talking to a small figure sitting beside the bed. She stood up when she heard them approach and walked toward them, her face a picture of exhaustion.

"Doctor Brown, I'd like to introduce someone to you."

The doctor looked less than interested as her tired eyes turned to Paulie. "Pleased to meet you," she lied, holding out a limp hand.

Paulie felt desperately sorry for someone who was clearly operating beyond the bounds of reasonable endurance. "Sorry to disturb you, we'll be going now," she said.

"Tell her where you're from," Green prompted. He was obviously a man to whom empathy was a foreign country.

Paulie sighed but decided that the quickest way out of this was to play along. "I'm from Arbroath, Kalama County."

The doctor's eyes brightened a little. "Really? Is it true that you've established law and order there? And a hospital?"

Paulie's mind flitted to images of her rag tag group of deputies and the medical room in the basement of the department store and shook her head. "From what I've seen here, you're doing at least as well as we are."

"I'm not so sure about that," Brown said. "Folks here don't feel secure—we've been raided before and it's only a matter of time before it happens again."

"The sheriff is going to give me some advice on security, Gladys," Green said. "I'm sure it's better for people to remain here than to head out onto the roads. Safety in numbers and all that."

The patient in the bed behind them moaned.

"Look, I've got to get back to my patients. Come back later, will you? I'd like to know how things are out there," Brown said.

She put her hand out again and Paulie shook it. "Sheriff Paulina Ramos," she said.

"What? Ramos? Your name's Ramos?"

Puzzled, Paulie gave a little shrug and nodded.

"Well, I suppose it's a common enough name, but you never know."

"You never know what?"

Brown drew in a deep breath. "You don't know a Luna Ramos, do you? She said her mom's a deputy."

"What?!" Paulie shrieked.

The little figure sitting beside the bed stirred, awoke and looked up.

"Mommy!" She leaped up and threw herself into Paulie's arms as the sheriff swung her around, their tears mingling as they whirled.

Luna pulled herself back, her face puffed up and wet. "Mommy, Uncle Alejandro, he's sick, real sick."

Paulie caught the eye of the doctor. Brown gave a small shake of the head, and the tears came again.

CHAPTER 16

SOLLY

SOLLY AND ROSS HAD headed west as fast as they could manage after their escape from Wright-Patterson Air Force Base. The gunfire had been dying down as Solly had returned to their quarters to find Ross ready to go, having packed all their gear.

Their pickup had been parked nearby and Solly's plan was to wait for the Lee Corp fighters to retreat and then try to sneak out in the chaos that followed it, using the rips they'd made in the perimeter fence to escape through.

They drove the car to the edge of the base building complex and waited for the telltale whip-whip-whip of helicopter blades spinning up. As soon as he saw the navigation lights rising, he stabbed his foot on the gas and half slid his way over the broken chain link, praying that they weren't running over razor wire. It was a desperate chance, but it worked and, aside from the odd stray round cracking off into the night around them, they were able to make their escape across the airfield and find an open gate to accelerate through.

Once they'd gotten away, Solly was determined to put as many miles as possible between them and any pursuers. The first part of the journey went quickly, as the military had cleared the roads of vehicles, but they soon got bogged down again and were forced to take shelter in the small town of Richmond, IN, less than sixty miles from the base. Solly wanted to get below ground so that they could examine the cylinder. He'd been treating it as if it were a loaded weapon ever since he'd been told it had a mind, imagining it was some sort of super smart Alexa. It lay in its shielding, stowed at the bottom of his bag in the trunk, just in case it could hear them talking.

So, they'd left the pickup in a dark corner of the underground parking lot at the local mall. They'd seen a few people as they drove into town, but there was no sense of an organized community here and no sign of life in the parking lot—probably explained by the overwhelming stench.

They parked the car beside a stairwell on the bottom floor, took their packs out and, flashlights at the ready, forced the "Staff Only" door open. With a sigh of relief, Solly drew air into his lungs and smelled nothing more odious than a faint aroma of oil and floor polish.

"Here, an office," he said and opened the door onto what once must have been the hub of a little empire. The flashlight swept the walls, revealing calendars, staff schedules, employee of the month awards with photos of smiling recipients, and down onto a tidy table with a three-tier letter tray. Solly imagined a small and neatly dressed man or woman sitting in the worn out office chair, lecturing one of their subordinates on timekeeping. In another world only weeks away.

Solly sat in the chair, pulled the cylinder from his pack and laid it on the desk beside a tiny stress toy in the shape of a dinosaur that, Ross discovered, did unmentionable things when it was squeezed.

"Come on, Ross," Solly grumbled, handing his flashlight to the boy to hold. "This is serious."

He rolled the cylinder back and forth until he found a seam that ran along the length of the shielding that had been added at the base. It looked like a silver foil, but, on closer inspection, Solly could see that it was translucent and crisscrossed by lines of fine wire. As he nudged at the seam, he noticed that it was held together by nothing more than Velcro, so he took a letter opener from the desk and began prying the two sides apart.

"Look at that," he said.

He'd expected to find that, once the shielding had been removed, the device was more or less unchanged, though he'd hoped to see some evidence of the claims made by the scientist from the base lab that it was "alive."

In fact, Brendon had removed the original surface of the cylinder which, as it turned out, was merely a protective skin. Gone was the smooth metal finish to be replaced by an intricate mesh of embedded wires covering the entire device save for one area of black glass that, presumably, functioned as a display. More than anything else, it reminded Solly of the handle of a light saber.

"What does it say?" Ross said, "Look, right there, writing."

Solly brought the device up close. "It says ALISON. Some sort of acronym, I imagine. Well, at least we know what it's called.

Hello, I am Alison. Are you my father?

Solly leaped out of the chair and, with an involuntary spasm, dropped the device onto the table where it rolled into the base of the letter tray.

"It spoke!" he said to Ross. "You heard it, didn't you?"

Ross, who'd flattened himself against the inside of the door, nodded mutely.

Solly crept back to the table and rolled the device gingerly back toward the front of the desk. It came to rest with the display facing him.

Are you my father?

A pixelated eye made up of cyan dots scrolled onto the black display, then settled there, moving back and forth as if searching for something.

It's dark in here. I'm frightened.

There was nothing else for it, but to play along. He'd talked to Siri and Alexa often enough, after all.

"Who are you?" The real question he'd wanted to ask was "What are you?" but that somehow felt inappropriate.

My name is Alison. Who are you?

"I'm called Solly."

Are you my father? I am not supposed to talk to strangers.

Solly paused for a moment. If he answered "no," the device would probably lock itself and not respond to his questions. On the other hand, lying didn't come easily to Solly Masters—a weakness that had gotten him into trouble more than once over the years. But then again, this was only a machine and, after all, Solly wasn't Ross's father, genetically speaking, but he took parental responsibility for the boy despite that.

"Yes, Alison, I'm your father," he said, shooting a glance at Ross and shutting down his retort before he had a chance to say anything.

Oh good. Where are we, father?

"We're in the basement of a car park in Richmond, Indiana."

Is the key here?

"No." Solly had no idea what the key might be, but it certainly wasn't here. "Do you know where it is?"

No. I need it, but that's all the information I've been given.

"Don't worry, we believe the key is in Arbroath and we're heading there at the moment."

Hooray! I'm so happy to have met you, father. Or would you like me to call you daddy?

"Father will do," Solly said. "Time to go to sleep—do you know how I deactivate you?"

Silly father. I go to sleep all by myself: if you'll tell me a story.

And so Solly Masters sat in the dark and recounted the tale of the Three Little Pigs to a glowing metal tube until it dimmed and went out.

"AM I THE ONLY one who's freaking out?" Ross said as they got back on the road. They'd spent the remainder of the night in that little office because it was moonless and Solly didn't want to be driving through a strange town in the dark lit up like a mobile lighthouse. As soon as the lights had gone out, he'd wrapped the cylinder in its sheath as he suspected this would keep it in a deactivated state until, if ever, they chose to open it again.

"I can promise you, telling a story to a smartspeaker, rather than the other way around, ranks as possibly the weirdest moment of my life, and it's had a lot of competition over the past couple of months."

They turned onto a road heading north and Ross wound down the window, filling the car with chilly but wonderfully fresh air. "It was the eye that was the weirdest thing. I thought I was Frodo on top of Amon Hen."

"'Take it off! Fool, take it off! Take off the Ring!'" Solly said, and the two of them laughed as the car picked a path along the highway heading north, united in geekdom on a sunny winter's day.

It was only a brief respite, however. As soon as the sounds of their laughing and chatting were replaced by the rush of the wind through the open window and the truck's diesel engine, his mind began to pick again at the mystery of the cylinder.

Whatever else Alison might have been, one thing was obvious—she was a child. He didn't know how that could have been possible in an artificial being, but he'd reconciled himself to not learning a lot from her. He hoped he wouldn't live to regret deciding to impersonate her father. What if she discovered the lie? He was reminded again of Alison's resemblance to a lightsaber and found himself wondering if she might prove to be a similarly powerful weapon. After all, given how important she seemed to be, this was the only explanation. A second wave was coming and she, he was told, could stop it—that only made sense if she had some destructive power to oppose the Lee Corporation.

"Where are we heading for?" Ross said as they found a clear section of highway and picked up speed.

"I want to go north before turning west," Solly responded. "So, I'm heading for Chicago and we'll pass it on the south. Then it's just a matter of going west until we get there. If we hit the sea, we've gone too far."

They made good progress that day and spent the night in a motel room in Lafayette. This time, they chose the upper floor, but the first room they went into was already occupied by the dead, so they found the closest one that looked over the parking lot. They'd seen some traffic on the road as they'd headed north, all of it moving toward Chicago and, as they watched, a car turned into the lot and drew up next to their truck.

"I'll deal with this," Solly said. "You stay out of sight."

"I'm getting fed up with you saying that. We're supposed to be partners," Ross said to Solly's retreating back.

A man was standing beside the truck looking into the cabin. His handgun swung around to face Solly, who'd called from the cover of a low brick wall in front of the motel.

The man put his weapon on the roof of the truck and raised his hands. "I don't mean no harm," he called. "It's just me, my lady and a baby. We're headin' north. Looking for somewhere to stay the night. We can move on if this is your place."

Solly watched as a young woman got out of the car holding a baby.

"Get back in, Martha, it ain't safe," the man hissed.

Solly stood up and tucked his weapon into a pocket of his coat before walking cautiously toward them.

"If you really don't mean any harm," he said, "then you're welcome. We've only just got here."

The man looked around as if searching for others. "We?"

Solly nodded. "Me and... my son." There, he'd said it.

"My name's John Baptiste," the man said, relaxing as he walked forward, hand extended. "It's good to meet a friendly face."

Solly took his hand. "Solly Masters."

"That there is Martha," he said, pointing at the woman with the baby. "And little Jenson."

"Your wife and son?"

Baptiste's face registered surprise and then sadness. "No. I found Martha when I was passin' through Denver. She had the little one with her."

"Jenson's the son of my old neighbors and I couldn't just leave him there when I found them passed away. John saved me."

"Ah, I just did what any right-minded person would do," Baptiste said, his pale skin coloring.

Solly gestured toward the motel. "You're welcome to stay here. It'd be good to have some conversation. Where are you headed? Chicago?"

"We're going to Virginia," Martha said as she walked into the dark hotel lobby.

"Why?"

Baptiste turned in surprise. "We're answering the call."

"What?"

"The call to arms. Haven't you heard? There's a president in DC again. The government's back."

KHALED LAY ON HIS bed in the white cell, looking up at the ceiling and watching imaginary patterns forming, moving and disappearing. He'd been left entirely alone today, unlike yesterday when Commander Chen had been triumphantly exhorting him to join her on the winning side.

He sighed as he remembered the good old days when she was simply Lia Chen, Chief Administration Officer of Lee Corporation and utter devotee of Annabel Lee. On the rare occasions he'd seen her, she'd struck him as a clever, capable, woman, though perhaps frustrated that she'd reached a glass ceiling because administration wasn't going to offer her a route to the very top of the tree. Well, she'd certainly solved that problem. The chief security officer had disappeared in suspicious circumstances and Lia Chen was promoted to replace him.

This had all happened six months or so before the Long Fall and she now headed what was, in practice, a private army.

"You take stubbornness too far," she'd said yesterday. Khaled had revealed nothing under interrogation. Frankly, their attempts to intimidate him were pathetic for a man who'd been subject to the tender ministrations of the Egyptian police in his youth. He suspected that they still valued him and wanted to learn what he knew while inflicting the minimum damage, but he'd managed to resist so far. What did he care about himself? He'd lost just about everyone that mattered to him.

So, Chen had visited him. "But we will succeed despite your resistance to our questions," she'd continued. "You see, we know that you arranged for something to be smuggled out of the building, and we know where it went. We lost it for a while but, I'm delighted to say, we have found it again. And, tonight, I am sending an entire squad with helicopter support to retrieve it. I guarantee they will not fail."

They had. This was obvious by Chen's absence from his cell today. She suspected that Khaled wasn't the only employee working against her, and the opportunity to gloat in front of the person she saw as the ring leader of this resistance would have been too great to resist. Somehow, then, Solly and Neil had gotten away with the device or, at least, Khaled had to hope that it was them, as seemed likely. Neither knew what it truly was, but he'd impressed on Neil how essential it was for it to get into the hands of the man calling himself Pastor Smith on the northwestern coast.

Alison. It had been Scott Lee's passion project for many years arising, Khaled suspected, from his frustration that Annabel had no interest in having children with him. He'd kept it from her for that very reason and the project had remained secret until a few months before the Long Fall when Scott had revealed it to Khaled and thus drawn him into the conspiracy to fake his death.

Even Khaled didn't understand the full implications of Alison. He only hoped that the project wasn't, in truth, merely a way for Scott to play happy families with an imaginary child. There was, of course, the other one—the one modeled entirely on Annabel Lee herself, the one the Lee Corporation knew all about. He hoped never to encounter that model. The last thing this shattered world needed was the return of the person responsible for its destruction.

Chapter 17

Paulie

ALEJANDRO DIED THAT EVENING. Paulie was there when it happened and so, at her insistence, was Luna who, though only ten years old, had made her point of view crystal clear. Alejandro had looked after her for the past seven weeks and she wanted to be there for him, even though he couldn't possibly know. Neither of them noticed it happen. One moment they were nodding off, arms wrapped around each other in an easy chair, the next minute Luna and Paulie were both sobbing.

"Why couldn't you come quicker?" she wailed. "I texted you, I even prayed, but you didn't come."

Paulie's heart sank and a black shroud descended. She'd received one of Luna's messages when she'd connected her smartphone to power weeks ago, but she'd had no way of knowing when it had been sent and had felt duty bound to stay in Arbroath. Now she knew she'd been wrong. She should have gone that day, driven down to LA, found the two of them and brought them back with her. Alejandro would now be alive, and her daughter wouldn't hate her. Fear had stopped her getting on the road south—fear that she'd find out for certain her daughter was dead. She vowed never to let it rule her again.

It was an 85-mile drive north from Johnson Green's community back to Arbroath, and Paulie wanted to cover that distance in a single day, so they set off as dawn arrived. Green emerged from the main building, half dressed with mist steaming from his mouth, and implored her not to go.

"You told me that there are dozens, perhaps hundreds, of people on the road heading for my town. I need to get there before they do, or they risk being turned away. In any case, that's where I belong."

And that was that. She felt a pang of regret as it seemed to her that, unlike the toxic community she'd spied on in Seattle, this was a true example of what was possible if people with good intentions came together. Arbroath was another, and that was where she was heading.

It had taken every ounce of determination to get Luna into the front seat of the car that morning. In fact, it was only Dany's presence, leaning over from the back and nuzzling the girl's ear, that persuaded the child to acquiesce.

Luna had wanted to see Alejandro buried in the little community graveyard and, to be truthful, so did Paulie, but there was no time to delay. Having seen the ugly side of her own people only the previous week, she did not want to leave their reaction to chance when refugees started appearing on their doorstep. Most of the folk inside the walls had no inkling of what it was like out here and what drove others to walk the dangerous roads north to their town. Arbroath, it seemed, was a beacon, and it was drawing people from far and wide.

The first half of the road north was familiar as Paulie had traveled down it over the previous couple of days, but fifty miles in they hit a fork and headed into less familiar territory. Almost as soon as they moved onto I-20, the obstructions increased, and the way became much harder to find.

They passed little groups of people moving in the same direction as them and, at one stage, she was forced to draw her pistol to face down a man trying to get a lift for himself and the two women who were with him. They looked exhausted, but Paulie knew that, if she stopped for them, she would probably get stuck as others begged for assistance. No, it was better to make sure that they got the help they needed when they arrived. If they made it.

The sky was beginning to darken as they approached Arbroath. Luna's sobbing episodes had decreased in frequency, and she had told Paulie what had happened after the Long Fall. Alejandro had, at first, insisted on them staying in his apartment. He had good stocks of food and had seen the riots breaking out in the streets below and, in any case, he knew that Paulie would look there first when she came to find them.

But then their food had run out. He went scavenging and, on the final occasion, returned with a knife slash to his thigh. He decided that LA wasn't safe for her any longer, so they walked to the outskirts, and he found a car. Luna cried when she said he'd put a blanket over the seat where the dead woman had been for Luna to sit on. They had intended to go to Arbroath, but Alejandro became sick and so, when they found Johnson Green's community, they stopped there, and he'd been in bed ever since. Sepsis, the doctor had said. And not enough antibiotics to kill it off.

Despite the tears that cascaded down both their cheeks—Paulie's a mixture of grief and shame—she was relieved that Luna was at least talking about things now.

Suddenly, as they crested a low hill, Paulie saw the light glint off something metallic ahead and slammed on the brakes, pulling in between two abandoned cars. She got out of the car, crouching low and creeping along the row of rotting metal to the front and peering over the hood. They were above Arbroath here and this road led to the bridge that crossed the river before arriving at the rear barricade into the town.

Halfway down the hill sat a group of military vehicles facing toward Arbroath, as if to prevent anyone heading south from it. She didn't need the layabout attitude of the men standing around the vehicles to know that they belonged to the militia from Seattle. Could they have followed the pastor and the others when they returned to Arbroath? Could they have been captured and forced to reveal where they'd come from?

How was she to get into town now? She was willing to bet that the main road along the river would also be blockaded which left only one option.

She reversed the car until they found a side road that took them to the west. They turned north and shadowed the highway, hoping that the militia were too lazy to scan the neighboring roads, until they reached the intersection that took them back onto the interstate as it went over the bridge.

"You need to get down, Luna," Paulie said. "There might be guards up there and I intend to drive straight through them."

Luna's face was a mix of terror and excitement as she folded herself into the foot well, her hand reaching back to hold the dog's head down.

"Ready?"

The little girl nodded. Paulie drew in a deep breath and stabbed her foot on the gas.

The car lurched up the final rise and flew out onto the highway, skidding round and, in one perfectly executed arc, straightening. Two men struggled to get onto their feet, kicking over the little fire where they'd been sharing a cigarette. By the time they'd brought their rifles to bear, Paulie was past them and half way across the bridge.

Pellets of glass blew over Paulie's shoulders as the rear window exploded, and then they were off and away, heading into the deserted suburbs of Arbroath.

"Are you alright?" she called over the sound of rushing wind.

Luna looked up, brushing the shattered glass from her clothes and face, and nodded.

Dany barked from the back seat and tried to climb over into the front.

"Get back, girl," Luna said as she hugged the dog's head.

The direct route to the enclave was to the right where another bridge took them over the Wishkah

River, but she was certain she'd find more militia there, so she drove north through the suburbs to a small crossing of the river as it bent westwards. She was then able to loop around to the east and approach the enclave from above.

She parked and walked to the lookout point, Luna and Dany tagging along beside her.

"There it is," Paulie said, pointing down to where the barricade stood, with its makeshift gate in the center. She looked to the left and cursed. A tank, two military trucks and an olive green jeep were parked to one side. It looked as though they'd only just arrived because the militia were busy setting up what looked like gun emplacements and mortar positions. It was an obvious show of strength intended to intimidate.

She watched as a familiar figure climbed down from the jeep and walked toward the gate. Almost immediately, it opened to admit a lone man. It was Scott Lee, still impersonating a Pastor judging by the Bible shaped object he held clutched to his chest.

So, he'd made it back safely which meant that Marvin and Jon had also returned, with any luck. But she could see no way out of this—they'd failed in their mission to scavenge heavier armament and five minutes under the hail of bullets from the machine guns now trained on the barricade and it would burst asunder.

Smith held out his hand and, with obvious reluctance, the man he'd said was called Lad Melua, head of security for the Lee Corporation, shook it. After no more than a moment or two, he withdrew and began talking animatedly to Smith. Dany growled softly but stopped at a word from Luna.

Through all of this, the pastor remained impassively listening and then, as Melua paused awaiting a response, he opened the Bible. Paulie half expected the idiot to draw out a handgun, shoot his opponent, and then die in a hail of bullets. In that instant, she was surprised to note that she didn't want that to happen.

Instead of that, he drew out something too small for Paulie to see. It must have been no larger than a credit card and Melua took it instantly, before suddenly bringing it close to his face as if he couldn't believe what he was seeing. He seemed to be looking back and forth from the object to the pastor before he started speaking, the words tumbling out, a mixture of surprise and, unless Paulie was quite mistaken, pleasure. For an instant, he moved as if to embrace Smith, but he stopped himself, returned the card, turned on his heels and left.

He spoke to his men, and, after much shaking of heads, they piled into their trucks and headed away. Within ten minutes, the way was clear of vehicles and a cheer went up from inside Arbroath. If that wasn't inexplicable enough, she looked back to the road to see that they'd left the machine guns in place and a group of deputies, led by Jon Graf, were striding out to retrieve them. Unable to hold back her curiosity any longer, Paulie straightened up, went back to the car and drove down to the riverside road that led to the barricade.

It took a while to get anyone's attention as she parked the car at the entrance to Arbroath. She was forced, in the end, to stab down on the horn repeatedly until a head popped up, followed by a leveled shotgun.

It was Marvin, so she got out especially carefully until he could see her face clearly.

"Sheriff!" he called with unmistakable joy. "Well, I'll be. Come on over!"

He called to someone behind him, and a ladder was lowered as Paulie went around and got her pack and Luna's from the trunk. She sent her daughter up first, then passed up the luggage. She was forced to put her shoulder under Dany's backside to get her up the ladder, before finally following her over the top.

Nothing had changed, on the surface at least, since they'd departed on their ill-fated mission to Seattle the previous week. As she stood on the barricade, people who'd been gathered around the market square detached themselves and began moving, some of them running. Paulie, delighted by the welcome, saw that they'd been looking at the machine guns. Smith remained beside the new weapons, watching the crowd before looking up at her.

She climbed down and was engulfed. "Where have you been?" was the most common question among the greetings and the back slapping. Mayor Vogelbach pushed through to the front and grabbed her hand.

"I'm so pleased you've returned to us, just as the pastor has delivered us from our enemies" she said. "And I see you've brought some new residents."

Paulie pulled Luna forward. "This is my daughter. Luna, this is Mayor Vogelbach."

Luna took the mayor's offered hand briefly. "My uncle's dead."

"I'm sorry to hear that," Vogelbach said. "You're safe now."

"This is Dany. She protects us. Uncle Jon!" Luna shrieked as Deputy Graf forced his way through. She jumped into his arms and Paulie was overwhelmed by the joy and love the two exchanged. He was twirling around, tears flowing down his face, and she knew that he was crying for joy and for grief at the same time. What a twisted world they were living in.

Paulie extricated herself from the crowd and strode across to Smith.

"I'm glad you made it back," he said, with every sign of meaning it.

She looked around to make sure they couldn't be overheard.

"What happened at the gate?" she said, watching his expression closely. "And don't play dumb; I was watching from the lookout point. I saw you hand something over."

He considered this for a moment before responding, "It was my Bible."

"Is that what you told them," she said, gesturing at the crowds still chattering by the barricade. "Did you say it was a miracle?"

Smith shrugged. "Does it matter? The end result is the same. The enemy has gone, and we are now armed to defend ourselves. One machine gun emplacement at each entrance and no one can approach us without permission."

"Let me see your Bible," she said, holding out her hand.

He reached into his pocket and retrieved a black book with gold lettering. "Here."

She flicked through the pages. "This isn't the same one. I saw you pull something out of it and show it to Melua. I want to know what it was, and why it made him turn on his heels and leave. Anyone would think you were on the same side."

"I persuaded him that he would find softer targets elsewhere."

Paulie shook her head. "I don't buy it. He had machine guns, mortars and a tank, for heaven's sake. What do we have? A few shotguns. No way. Now tell the truth or I'll have you arrested."

"That would be a mistake," Smith said.

She spotted Deputies Friedman and Fessel. "Nicky, Mike, come over here, will you?" she called.

"I want you to arrest the pastor and throw him in the holding cell."

Friedman looked from one to the other. "This a joke, right?"

"I'm giving you a direct order," Paulie said, wondering just how deep this man's influence on the town now reached.

The two deputies shared a glance and stepped back. "Sorry, Sheriff," Fessel said. "The pastor's just saved us and I reckon we might get lynched if we arrest him."

"Now you listen to me," Paulie hissed. "You either take my orders or lose your badges"

"I'd rather lose my badge than my neck. You might want to hightail it back to wherever you've been if you don't like the pastor; folks here won't tolerate it, I'm tellin' you," Fessel said.

Paulie couldn't believe her ears. "I'll deal with you two later," she snapped, before drawing her weapon and pointing it at Smith. "Come with me, Pastor."

Smith's forehead creased into a frown as the crowd slowly went silent. "I'm so sorry, Paulie. You really should have thought about this a little. Mike, will you please escort the sheriff to the cell."

"What's going on?"

Paulie turned to see Jon Graf hurrying toward her, Luna running along beside him.

"She's fixin' to arrest the pastor," Fessel said.

"What?"

"I can't explain, Jon, not in front of everyone. Now, will you please take him into custody."

"He's just saved the town!" Graf said, disbelief obvious.

"Jon, please."

He held her gaze for a few moments, then shook his head and stepped back.

"Mommy, what's happening?" Luna called.

"I wish I knew."

The pastor pushed the weapon she was pointing away from him. "I think we all need time to calm down. Please go with the deputies."

She had no choice, especially with Luna watching. "You stay with Uncle Jon," she said, while treating Graf to a venom laced glance. "I'll see you soon enough." She began moving toward the Sheriff's Office.

Suddenly, Dany began barking and baring her teeth at Fessel. She jumped up and pushed him sideways with her front paws.

"Get down, Dany," Paulie said. "Go with Luna, protect her."

"What's goin' on?" Melvin Tucker burst out of the crowd and barged into Friedman. "Put your weapons down you damn fools. What are you doin' pointin' them at the sheriff?"

"Stand down, Melvin," Jon called, "the sheriff's under arrest."

"Like hell I will," he responded, standing between the two deputies and Paulie. "You should be ashamed'a yourselves after all she's done for this town!"

Graf drew his sidearm and the crowd that had gathered retreated a little. "Hand over your weapon, deputy. You can share a cell with the sheriff."

Paulie looked at Marvin and nodded. The last thing she wanted was a firefight to break out in the middle of a crowd with her daughter looking on.

Paulie walked through a disbelieving mob that was filled with hostility. So, after all her work to bring stability and safety to the town, this was how she was rewarded? Treachery from those she most trusted and loyalty from the person she least expected to be on her side.

She'd lost the one place she considered safe, the place she'd brought her child to, the place she'd have given her life to protect. The world was truly, utterly, messed up.

Chapter 18

Bella

Bella did her best impression of an infantryman crawling stealthily through the detritus. In truth, she knew she'd have looked ridiculous to anyone who happened to be watching but she didn't care. After much squeezing, rolling and pushing, she found a vantage point over the intersection where her father had been taken hostage.

The days since she'd left the airbase had been the loneliest of her life. Guilt, shame and powerless rage took turns to be the dominant emotion as, with every mile, she felt more and more as though she was abandoning her children. She'd seen neither since Nathan had slipped her that pass and her mind had settled on the one remaining mission, the thing she could do—find out what had happened to her father.

She expected to find that he was dead, dispatched once that thug Skulls realized that the old man couldn't repair the wind turbine. One way or another, she needed to know, so she squinted through the sights of the hunting rifle. That had been one piece of luck; she'd found the rifle in a remote cabin where she'd sought shelter the previous night. She'd also been lucky to slip by the guards at the TLX border. As Nathan had suggested, she'd shadowed the main interstate, but she hadn't wanted to stray too far as she had no idea where she was and didn't want to lose sight of the arterial road. It was only when she'd passed the border that she realized she'd been in full view of the checkpoint as it was on an elevated section of the highway. If a guard had been looking, they'd have had no difficulty in spotting her.

Bella saw Skulls almost immediately as he moved back and forth chatting to his confederates and giving orders. The man's swagger hadn't lessened, though now he wore a blue cap on his bald head which, with his yellow beard, gave him the look of a cartoon seaman. All he needed was a pipe.

She watched for an hour, seeing many people, but never her father. Finally, she had to accept that he wasn't going to appear and that her worst fears had been realized. She focused on Skulls, imagining what it would be like to gently squeeze the trigger and take revenge for Al's death. If it hadn't been for the fact that Maddie was being held captive in TLX, Bella would have done it even if it had meant every other scumbag descended upon her.

But she had to survive for her daughter's sake, she was the child's only hope. So, she relaxed her grip and went to put the rifle down, but it slipped forward a little on the damp ground. Reflexively, she grabbed at it, accidentally squeezing the trigger. With a crack, the gun kicked back and landed on the ground. Bella cursed as she scrambled away on all fours before getting to her feet and running.

She'd been sure the safety was on—what sort of idiot leaves it off in their gun cabinet?

The car was just there, and she drew in deep breaths as she went to open the front door.

"Hold it right there, lady," said a drawling voice. "I want a word with you."

Skulls grabbed her arm and propelled her down the bank toward the intersection. She struggled against his iron grip as the others laughed at her discomfort.

"Looks like we're gonna have ourselves a little entertainment, boys," Skulls cried as Bella stumbled down to the road where they'd been hijacked.

"What are you going to do with me?" she said.

Skulls gave an evil chuckle. "Well, you're just gonna have to wait to find out, aren't ya? You nearly took off my head."

"I didn't mean to, I was putting the gun down!"

"Maybe that's right, maybe it ain't," Skulls said.

"Believe me, if I'd intended to kill you, you'd be dead right now," Bella spat, anger overcoming fear for a moment.

Skulls laughed again and pushed her toward a streetlamp that had a chair at its base and a noose hanging down.

"No!" Bella cried, tears welling in her eyes.

But Skulls pushed her past the makeshift gallows and into the parking lot of a car dealership then in through the front doors.

"Hey boss!" he called out as he maneuvered her toward the former manager's office. "Look what the cat caught."

Skulls pulled her to a halt and waited.

Bella stood, panting as she waited for judgement to be pronounced.

A figure appeared in the doorway, silhouetted by the sun coming in through the office window. A familiar figure.

"Thank God!"

"Dad!"

She threw herself into his arms and wept until she felt as though she'd run dry. He pulled back and looked at her, his eyes red with tears. Then he looked behind her. "Isabella, where are the kids?"

Al wouldn't tell her his story until she'd told him hers and she watched his old and wrinkled face turn pale as she described what had happened to Maddie.

He thought for a moment before shaking his head. "Well, I suppose it makes sense —"

"What?" Bella burst out.

Al held his hand up. "Hold on, I was going to say that it makes sense if you think of people as cattle. To rebuild a population, you'd want to pair people up."

"But she's only fourteen!"

"I know," Al said. "But her most fertile years are just around the corner, it's a fact of nature."

Bella leaped up, spilling her chair backwards onto the floor, and went to stand at the window. "Are you suggesting we leave her there? Because she'll be cared for? Like a brood mare?"

"Don't be ridiculous, Isabella. Haven't you got the brains you were born with?"

"But you just said—"

Al joined her at the window. "I said I understand what they're doing, not that I agree with it. No, we need to get our girl out of there."

"Dad," Bella said, putting her arm around the old man's shoulder. "Why are you still alive? I thought they'd kill you for sure."

Al grunted. "So did I, to be honest, but I soon worked out that Skulls hadn't been lying when he said they're not murderers. They're a load of klutzes, and he's the brightest of them, which isn't saying a lot."

"But there's a lynching post out there!"

"It's just for show. Skulls had the brains to know that they wouldn't survive long if they didn't look like they were tough, but he's a good boy, really."

Bella whistled in amazement. "And did you get the turbine working?"

"I did, though it's only really good for powering the lights and we're careful not to overuse them—don't want to attract any trouble. Notice that they've cleared the road? No more traps?"

"I hadn't, actually, I was a bit preoccupied."

"Well, we're making our way legitimately now, real trading and scavenging. Folks stop and we give them what they need in exchange for anything they've got to trade."

"What if they haven't got anything?"

Al smiled. "Then they get what they need anyway. Took a while to persuade Skulls it was the right thing to do, but we got there."

"Dad, why do they follow you?"

"Because, my daughter, Skulls is just bright enough to know he's stupid and the others follow his lead. Besides, they get coffee now—I got the machine working again. Gives the batteries a pounding, but worth every amp. Now, let's go find Skulls and then we'll go get our Maddie back."

BELLA, AL AND SKULLS headed west the following morning. Al had been uncomfortable bringing Skulls along because that left the little community at the intersection with the combined intellectual capacity of a fifth grader, but the big man had insisted. Bella, in turn, hadn't wanted Al to come because of his age and because she'd only just discovered he was alive. And Skulls hadn't wanted a woman along on a mission that was, obviously, man's work. So, they made for a motley crew as they drove along the highway in Skulls's favorite pickup.

Maddie was being held at a place called Cedar Ranch near Bulverde, TX, according to the orders they'd been given back at the base. Al, who'd stripped all of the cars that had been abandoned at the intersection, had a stack of route maps, so they soon discovered that Bulverde was to the north of San Antonio, and that meant a long drive, staying outside the TLX military area for as long as they could manage it. Al made notes on the map every time they came within sight of a checkpoint. In each case, as soon as they saw it, they reversed up the road and got onto the country lanes.

"They're only guarding the main interstates and highways," he said, once they'd been forced to do this for the fourth time. It looks to me as though they've created a protected zone around fifty miles east of San Antonio. I wonder why they're not covering the smaller roads."

Skulls, who was taking a turn at driving, shrugged. "Maybe they ain't got as many new recruits as they need."

"You're probably right," Al said.

Bella, who'd been watching from the back seat said, "They told me their first priority is security, so I guess Jake and others like him will be found manning a checkpoint on some country road before long."

"There's worse things he could be doing," Al responded.

THEY FOUND A ROADSIDE motel to sleep the night. Skulls, who seemed to have no fear of the dead, had swept through those rooms with doors that were shut and found two next to each other that were clear. Al and Bella took the first and Skulls the other.

Once they'd shut the drapes so they could light candles, Bella went into Skulls's room and found him sitting on the bed looking up at a painting on the wall above the headboard.

"Nice painting," Bella said.

"Yeh," Skulls said without taking his eye off it. The print showed the side view of a woman looking out of a window onto a wooded landscape. "It's a Hopper. Cape Cod Morning."

Bella's eyes widened. "Do you know a lot about paintings?"

Skulls shrugged. "It's a hobby. I like Hopper. Feel as though he has somethin' to say. That woman there: looks like my Freda."

"Who?"

He turned to her, and she saw the pain on his face. For the first time, she noticed the unfolded picture lying on the bed in front of him. A pretty woman in biker gear smiling to the camera.

"My lady," he said. "Gone now, o'course. What would she think of what I became? Just a thug."

Impulsively, Bella put her hands on his shoulders. "I'm sorry," she said. "Look, what should I call you? Skulls isn't your real name."

"It is now, Bella. Maybe I'll go back to being plain Steve one day, but not yet. Your pa, he saved me, turned me around."

Bella smiled. "He's gotten into the habit of doing that," she said. "Are you going to come into our room and have a bite to eat?"

With a nod, Skulls folded the little photo and slid it into his inside pocket. Bella followed him into the next room where her father was stirring a can of beans.

CEDAR PASS ROAD WAS a narrow lane with the entrances to farms and ranches on either side. Most appeared to have been constructed in the past few years, perhaps as the realization of long held dreams that were now nothing more than dust and ashes.

"That's it," Bella said. She was sitting in the passenger seat beside Skulls and could make out the stone sign.

Without warning, he slammed his foot on the brakes and immediately began reversing up the road, though he kept the engine's revs low, and they crept backward.

"What is it?"

"Guard," he hissed, pointing beyond the gate. Now Bella could see—a single figure walking back and forth with the unmistakable outline of a rifle pointing downwards.

They turned as soon as they could and took a side road that ran parallel to the ranch until it turned into a dirt track and then disappeared entirely.

"Good grief, they post guards on these women?" Bella said.

"No wonder they're short of sentries on the roads," Al responded from the back seat. "Still, we came to do a job, and I don't intend to leave this place without my granddaughter."

Bella turned to Skulls, who was scanning the surrounding woods and scrub. "What do you think?"

"If it was my daughter, I'd do anythin' to get her back."

"But she's not your daughter, so will you help?"

He turned to her, smiling. "Sure. Maybe time to make Freda proud of me."

Dusk was approaching as they crept toward the boundary of the ranch. Skulls led the way, carrying his sawn off shotgun, followed by Bella and Al who both had Glocks that had been liberated by Skulls's gang over the weeks.

Skulls climbed over a paddock fence and then helped the others down. The rear of the ranch was made up of a well cultivated garden that opened onto scrubbier land that retreated into the distance. Across the garden strode a figure, pacing to and fro as if in deep thought.

Bella took the lead now, gesturing to the others to follow her. If that was the mysterious "Ham" who owned the ranch, then he looked a lot younger than she'd imagined. She'd learned to recognize teenagers at long distance, and she wouldn't put this boy's age at above nineteen.

They reached the low brick wall that marked the garden's boundary and peered over. The boy approached another dark figure and took something from him before, to Bella's horror, walking directly toward them.

Crouching as flat to the wall as they could manage, they watched as the boy stood above them, a dark shape against the darkening sky, and lit a cigarette which flared orange before settling down again.

"I've got a gun and it's pointing right at your crown jewels," Al whispered. "Don't say a word. Just nod if you hear and understand."

The figure froze for a moment before nodding.

"Smoking's bad for your health, son," Al said as he got painfully to his feet, keeping his gun trained on the boy.

"We don't have nothin' here, and there's guards," he said in a trembling voice.

"Is Maddie here?" Bella asked.

Again there was a moment's pause before the boy spoke. "Yes."

"We're getting her out of here," Bella responded. "And you're going to help us—do you understand?"

She saw the boy's shoulders sag. "You can't get away. They'll be on you like a pack of dogs."

"Leave that to us," Bella said, sounding more confident than she felt. "Where is she?"

"In her bedroom, but you can't get to her. She's guarded."

Skulls loomed from behind a column of bricks. "How many guards?"

"Two at the moment. One's gone off shift."

"How many out back?"

"Just the one. Max."

"Now, why don't you just go tell that guard to go make a coffee?" Al said. "Don't play any tricks on me, son, you'll be in my sights all the way."

The boy's silhouetted head turned in his direction. "It won't work. I'm as much a prisoner as Maddie is."

"What?"

"Look, I'll help you, but you've got to take me with you, ok? And you've got to promise not to kill the guards."

Bella could hear Skulls's eyeballs rolling so she got in first. "We'll do our best, but they'll have to be incapacitated."

"You can lock them in the basement," the boy said. "Leave some food and water and they'll be fine until the next supplies drop in a few days."

"Sounds to me as though you've been plotting your escape for a while, son," Al said.

"More of a daydream, really."

Skulls jumped onto the lawn and Bella heard the boy gasp. "I'll be watching you, punk," he said. "Put a finger out of line and it'll be the last thing you do."

The boy nodded, and they followed him across the garden.

"Hide here," he said as they crouched against the back wall of the house. "I'll call Bob and you can grab him. But no killing, right? I like him."

The boy stepped into the shadows and called out the guard's name. Moments later, he appeared around the corner again, followed by a larger figure. Skulls leaped up and pressed the end of his shotgun barrel into the guard's chin.

Al held the man at gunpoint while the others tricked the guard around the front in the same way. They led them into the basement where the boy, whose name was Luke, locked them up. The guards evidently thought Luke was helping the invaders under duress, because neither protested at all.

Bella threw herself at Maddie when they found her. She'd been sitting up in bed, reading. Her face changed from a frozen kind of fear to utter joy as she recognized her mother and the two cried and twirled around as they hugged. Then Maddie saw her grandfather and the tears began again.

Luke came in, looking a little sheepish and Maddie disengaged from Al and embraced him as well, causing the boy's face to flush. "We have to get him out of here too, mom. He hates it."

"We sort of agreed to take him with us," Bella said, surprised by her daughter's obvious affection for the boy. "I didn't think you'd want a reminder of your imprisonment. I mean, he's the son of the man they were going to force you to marry."

Maddie shook her head. "No, that's not it at all. I was going to marry Luke. He hated the idea as much as me, but he's trapped too."

"We need to put a lot of miles behind us if we're to get away. If they catch us, they'll hang us all," Luke said.

Maddie ran around and packed her essentials before following the others out to the car. She gasped when she saw Skulls at the wheel.

"Don't worry none, " Al said as he opened the passenger door. "He's on our side."

They skidded away and, once they were out onto the country roads, Skulls turned off the car lights and drove by reflected moonlight.

Luke fell asleep almost instantly, his head on Maddie's shoulder and Bella smiled from the front seat. "Tell me about him. Did he lose everyone as well?"

Maddie shook her head. "No, he was lucky like us, though his father is a horrible man. We'd best hope he never finds us."

Bella went back to watching the road ahead and marveling at Skulls's ability to pick his way through in the dark.

"Mom," Maddie said softly, jerking Bella out of her half sleep. "We can't turn back now, can we?"

"Why, what have you forgotten?" Bella responded with a smile that died as she turned to look at her daughter's stricken face.

"Seriously, we can't go back, right?"

Bella shook her head. "No, we've come too far out into the country, we'd never find our way to the ranch and, anyway, that would be just heading for trouble."

"Good. You see, it's Luke's father. You need to know, and now's as good a time as any."

"What about him?"

There was a pause as Maddie summoned up the courage to speak.

"His name is John Murphy. Mom, he's the President of the TLX."

Chapter 19

Solly

THE SUN ROSE BEHIND them as they headed west toward Minneapolis. Solly and Ross had slept in a vacant car lot, wrapping themselves in blankets taken from the motel as the temperature dipped below freezing. Solly wanted to get around the city and back onto the interstate before it went dark again, so they'd been up and away early.

There was a government in Washington, DC and he was heading to another Washington on the other side of the country. Solly Masters had never been a political animal, but his heart had leaped at the thought of government being reestablished. There had been some official announcements in the hours and days after the Long Fall, but nothing since then, and he'd assumed the federal government was a thing of the past. Last he'd heard had been that someone called General Tusk had declared martial law.

John Baptiste—the man they'd met at the motel—had told them that there was a new civilian president who'd been appointed on the basis that she was the most senior surviving member of the old administration. Solly couldn't even remember her name, but he'd felt the hunger that had driven Baptiste to travel east. Solly's immediate future, however, lay to the west and then, once he'd discharged his duty, as he saw it, he would go south and lay to rest the likely ghosts of his family.

Baptiste had also told him that Texas and two other states had formed a new federation that was gathering a militia. This news had left him in two minds. On the one hand, he was glad to hear that some sort of order was being restored in his home state, but, on the other hand, forming an independent country was asking for a whole heap of trouble further down the line.

"Dammit!" he said, banging down on the steering wheel.

"What's the trouble?" Ross responded, startled out of sleep.

Solly sighed. "Sorry. I've spent too long in this truck and my mind's wandering. I feel like I need to be heading south and east, when I'm actually driving north and west."

"I know. You want to find out what happened to your family."

"Both my families, Ross," Solly responded.

"Do you miss Janice?"

A lump formed in Solly's throat as he thought of her. He'd done his very best to stop his mind wandering over the past few days but in the depths of the night he often saw her face. And then the guilt would build, followed by the fear that he'd left her and the children to fend for themselves while he went on a wild goose chase across the continent.

He felt so conflicted. How much simpler life would be if he had only one thing to think about, one responsibility to uphold. He wanted to go south to find Bella and the children, or back east to the farm which, now he was away from it, felt like home. And yet he was heading away from both and the invisible cord that bound him to those places was stretching tighter and tighter.

"Yes, Ross, I miss Janice. And the others."

"I miss Jaxon. I thought I was going to hate him, but he turned out okay. But wherever you plan on going, we're gonna need to pick up some gas today." He gestured at the fuel gauge.

Yes, that was the plan. They only had one jerrycan of diesel left, and Solly had pinpointed a series of rural gas stations on the route map for them to try, in the hope that at least one was still usable. They still had Landon's bailer bucket contraption in the trunk, so they wouldn't be reduced to siphoning from abandoned vehicles.

They finally struck lucky after noon. They'd passed three of Solly's targets, but two were burned out and the third was surrounded by vehicles arranged like a wall on all sides. Shots had rung out as they approached, and Solly had been forced to back up quickly and go another way.

This gas station, however, looked entirely deserted. They'd seen no signs of human life as they'd driven through small settlements, barging their way through where the road was still blocked by long abandoned vehicles. It reminded him of Sleeping Beauty—as if the kingdom had fallen asleep in an instant.

They rolled onto the forecourt and parked beside the one free pump, the other two blocked by cars that sat beneath a skin of dust. Snowflakes began to fall as they got out, carefully scanning the dark interior of the kiosk and the surrounding houses. It was as still and silent as a tomb.

"Where's the tank cover?" Solly asked as he scanned the ground.

Ross ran over to the side of the kiosk and came back with a large broom which he used to clear the leaves and dirt that had accumulated until he revealed a dull metal cover.

Solly fetched the bailer bucket and levered up the cover before reaching down and unscrewing the cap to the tank. He then lowered the bucket inside as Ross brought the first jerry can from the trunk, unscrewed the cap and dropped in a funnel.

"We've struck oil!" Solly said as the sloshing of the bucket echoed up out of the hole. "Now, let's see whether this thing works."

He pulled on the rope and lifted the tube out. "It's full!" Solly upended the bucket and carefully poured it into the jerrycan.

"Are you Ruskies?"

Solly was so startled he almost dropped the bucket. When he twisted around, he was looking into the barrel of a shotgun and, beyond it, stood an old man with trembling arms.

"No, we're from New York," Solly said, his voice trembling.

The old man spat as if to suggest that this was almost as bad an answer. He wore baggy jeans and a red checked shirt covered by a thick fur lined coat.

Watery eyes peeked out from behind round spectacles and his yellow stained white beard wagged as he chewed.

"You're not Ruskie spies, then? Sent to finish us off. Well, let me be tellin' you, I ain't surrenderin'. I did two tours of 'Nam and ten years as a deputy, and you can take my gun from my cold dead hands if you want to try. Are you feeling lucky?"

Solly had seen many examples of the mad and the bad since the Long Fall. The worst people he'd met had managed to combine the two. His mind flashed back to the fake religious leader in New York, and he wondered, in that instant, whether he had survived and what he was doing now. Seeking revenge for their escape, and the wound he suffered? But what of the Lee Corporation? They might have remained idle, but that didn't suit their style. What would they make of attempts to restore government in DC?

As for this man, he was definitely in the crazy camp, but, despite the quivering gun, Solly didn't see him as a threat—except accidentally.

"Sergeant, you can lower your weapon," he said, calmly.

The old man's eyes widened. "How'd you know I was a sergeant, sonny?"

Lucky guess, Solly thought. "Call it military instinct. Now, will you put the gun down? You're frightening the boy."

Glancing to the side, the old man shook his head as if to wake out of a dream and lowered the shotgun. "Sorry son. I didn't mean to alarm you."

Ross looked embarrassed and relieved at the same time.

"Sergeant Walter Hammond, 1st Brigade, 5th Infantry Division of the Red Devils," the old man said, popping a perfect salute.

Solly did his best to replicate it. "Solomon Masters, Special Operations," he said, tapping the side of his nose. Ross went to open his mouth, but Solly kicked his shins and the boy remained silent.

Solly and the veteran shook hands. "Sergeant, we need some diesel. We're heading west on a secret mission. Do we have your permission to resupply using your fuel dump?"

"Oh, yes indeed sir. I'll fetch the manual pump and we'll get it out of there easy as apple pie."

Another salute and the old man hobbled off to the rear of the kiosk.

"I guess we know why this place hadn't been raided before now," Solly said.

"He's a bit soft in the head, Sol," Ross replied. "Can we trust him?"

Solly nudged the boy in the ribs reproachfully. "You'd be a little addled if you'd gone through what he has and then, when you should be enjoying a quiet retirement chasing kids out of your pumpkin patch, the Long Fall happens. It wouldn't surprise me if he's got a shortwave radio tuned to a military frequency and heard the National Guard call up. Where has he gone?"

Solly and Ross walked around the back of the kiosk and found the old man rolling up a sleeping bag and stowing it in his pack.

"You've been living out here?" Solly gasped. Hammond's shelter amounted to the roof overhang and three garbage bins that had been rolled around it as a makeshift wall. "Why didn't you get inside?"

Hammond straightened up painfully. "It don't belong to me, that's why. I'm here to protect the fuel supply, not break into other folks' property."

"But it's freezing!" Ross said, gesturing at the snow that was now falling steadily.

"I'm pretty tough. Though it did get awful cold last night..."

"Sergeant, I give you official permission to use this kiosk as your sentry post."

The old man bent down to pick up a series of picture frames that had been laid in a row beside where he slept. "Thank you, sir, but that's no longer necessary."

"Why?"

Another salute. "Because I'm coming with you, sir."

"You can't let him come!" Ross said. They'd made camp beside the camping stove which they'd set up in the store room behind the kiosk. A large can of stewed beef was bubbling away, filling the room with a delicious aroma that set Solly's stomach rumbling.

"What do you suggest? You know he'll die if we leave him here."

"But he stinks! And he's mad!"

Solly turned to Ross. "I don't imagine we smell too sweet at the moment, and I don't think he's quite as crazy as I imagined at first. Some food and human company will hopefully bring him around a little. And anyway, he might be old—"

"He is old."

"—but he's a veteran. We could do with an extra pair of hands."

"You just love the fact that he thinks you're some sort of James Bond."

Solly laughed out loud. "Give it a rest. I mean, look at me. Do I look like Jack Reacher? John Milton?"

"You look a lot more like them than you did a few weeks back. Face it, Sol, you're not the man you once were."

"For better or worse," Solly said, shaking his head, though he felt a tinge of pride.

"We could just make a run for it while he's back at his house," Ross said, though without conviction.

Solly spooned a third of the can of stew into Ross's bowl and a third into his own. "Just enjoy your stew. And don't worry, you're still my second in command." He smiled and looked sidelong at Ross whose face flushed a little as he ate.

Solly reached into his bag and pulled out the cylinder. He'd discovered he could activate it without removing the outer wrap. What he hadn't worked out was why he felt so obsessed with activating it at all. He'd been talking to the device every night since it had spoken that first time. It was almost as if he half expected it to not answer one night. He wondered whether that would bother him and decided that it would. Now who was the crazy one?

Hello Father.

"Hello Alison."

Are we there yet?

"Now Alison, I told you it would take many weeks."

I know, but we seem to have been traveling for ages.

Solly looked down at the cylinder. Alison's lights could be seen through the semi-transparent silvered wrapping and he'd noticed that they reflected her mood—if a machine could have emotions. Right now, she was emitting a distinctly reddish tone.

"We've been refueling today," he said. "So we can travel faster tomorrow and the days after that."

I don't understand. What is fuel?

Maybe this was why he was so keen to talk to her every night. She asked questions he could actually answer with confidence. Alison reminded him of an empty mold—the shape existed, but there was nothing inside.

"What in the world is that?"

Solly snapped around to see Walter standing over him and Ross, pointing a shaking finger at the red pulsing thing in Solly's lap.

"It's a noo-clee-ar weapon, ain't it? What are you doin' with a noo-clee-ar weapon?"

"It's not a weapon," Solly said as he deactivated Alison and stowed the cylinder. "It's a computer. A bit like Alexa."

The old man rubbed his bearded chin. "Alexa? Isn't that the darned creepy thing that talks to you about the weather and suchlike? My grandson tried to get me one, but I told 'im I don't need no talking Pringles tube to tell me the weather when I can look outside my own door."

Hammond stopped for a moment, as if lost in memories. "Of course, he died when the Ruskies hacked them darned implants all the young folks got. I told 'em it would lead to a bad end. I'm seventy-eight and I've not had a day's sickness in my life. I wish he hadn't had to learn the hard way," the old man said, shaking his head sadly.

"This is a specialized version," Solly said, impressed that Hammond had worked out what had happened, even if blaming the Russians was going a bit too far. "We need to deliver it to our agent on the West Coast. It contains crucial intelligence."

"Oh, I see. Well, I'm with you. I've had a wash and brush up. I reckon I wasn't smellin' all that nice."

Solly glanced at Ross, and then up at Hammond. The beard was still there, though washed and trimmed, and the clothes looked like clean versions of those he'd been wearing.

Getting up, Solly took the old man's hand. "Glad to have you along, serg—"

His pack had begun to beep. Solly bent down and grabbed the cylinder. It was vibrating and flashing red.

Father. The beacon has been activated. Here is the message:

Her voice then deepened as if she was replaying a voicemail.

To the bearer of this device. Bring it to the following coordinates as soon as possible. Bring it soon or it will be too late. The fate of humanity depends on what you do over the next days. Hurry. The secret is out, and the enemy is hunting you.

Father.

The girlish voice had returned.

I'm frightened.

Solly nodded sadly. "So am I, Alison. So am I."

Epilogue

THE MAYOR OF FORT Brad, CA let out a loud snore and rolled over. His wife had long since found sanctuary in the bedroom furthest away from her husband and so he was the last to be woken up.

A hand reached down and shook the recumbent man's ample shoulders. "Mr. Mayor. Mr. Mayor!"

Luis Garcia sucked in a huge lungful of air, almost swallowing his tongue in the process, then floundered around, shaking his head to clear it of last night's tequila.

"*Como?* Who is it?" He leaned onto the bedside table to reach his spectacles, became suddenly aware of his nakedness and pulled the blankets up to his hairy shoulders. "Jones, is that you?"

"Yes, sir. Sorry to disturb you, but there's a situation on the beach."

Garcia was fully awake now, awake enough to be indignant. "On the beach? Look, Jones, if it's just some kids messing around on quad bikes again, I don't want to know."

"It's nothing like that, sir. Someone's coming ashore."

"What?"

"I think it's best you see for yourself, sir."

AND SO, MAYOR GARCIA was now in a police car smoothing his hair down with his hand and wondering what he'd done to deserve yet another emergency. He'd achieved the near impossible by uniting the remaining population and welcoming in those from neighboring towns to make a secure community. Geography had been on their side as Fort Brad was based around an old emplacement built during the wars of the 19th century and could only be approached from one direction.

He'd quickly galvanized the people, managing somehow to prevent the complete disintegration of order. His wife had to take some credit for helping with that—folk tended to do what she told them. Yeah, what a lucky stroke that she'd survived the Long Fall when everyone he cared about had died. Lucky.

The sun was just beginning to rise behind them as they approached the beach and Garcia could instantly see that something was seriously amiss. The tide was just starting to retreat, exposing acres of wet sand but whereas he'd expect to spot nothing more than a few people walking dogs or riding horses, what he actually saw reminded him more of one of those moving anthills from the South American rain forest.

The car bumped and slid a little as it left the slipway and headed across the sands. It was instantly illuminated by search lights that combed the beach, identifying the car and checking for any others. Perhaps he should have brought reinforcements.

A group of armed men was walking toward the car as it traveled over the sand.

"What shall I do, Mayor? Turn around?" The driver's voice was trembling.

Garcia felt like a rat in a trap. It was too late to do anything other than take the bait.

"No, pull up," he said.

Mayor Luis Garcia got out of the car and walked toward the approaching group. As they came within range of the car's headlights, he could see there was about a half dozen of them, most in camouflage fatigues, but led by a man in a peaked cap and light green uniform. Hundreds more were scurrying in the distant half-light.

They halted a few paces apart.

"Who are you?" Garcia said.

The man in the cap stepped forward briskly and Garcia saw another figure move with him, holding a camera.

"Do you represent the local authorities?" the officer said in clipped English with an American accent.

"I am the mayor."

The officer nodded curtly. "My name is Colonel Kun Sung-Jin of the Glorious Expeditionary Force. I claim this land on behalf of our dear leader."

Another man walked forward carrying a flag on a spiked pole. He handed it to his commander who raised it high and plunged it into the sand.

"You will return in one hour with any others who are required to make a lawful surrender."

Garcia's mouth had fallen open, and he stared at the man in wide eyed shock.

"Surrender to who?" he finally managed.

"To the army of the Democratic People's Republic of Korea."

Continue the story at books2read.com/longfall3

READ THE STRANGER

TWO WEEKS AGO, MILLIONS died in the space of a few hours, betrayed by the very technology that was supposed to bring an end to illness and misery.

Now a stranger makes a desperate journey across the United States to deliver hope to those who can fight back.

But many miles lie between him and the fulfilment of his mission.

When he arrives at a small town, he finds that his enemies are close behind. Can he escape and continue on his way, or will the Long Fall claim another victim?

Get it for free here: scrib.me/stranger or scan the QR code below.

Read The Stranger

Two weeks ago, millions died in the space of a few hours, betrayed by the very technology that was supposed to bring an end to illness and misery.

Now a stranger makes a desperate journey across the United States to deliver hope to those who can fight back.

But many miles lie between him and the fulfilment of his mission.

When he arrives at a small town, he finds that his enemies are close behind. Can he escape and continue on his way, or will the Long Fall claim another victim?

Get it for free here: scrib.me/stranger or scan the QR code below.

About Kev

READERS HAVE BEEN PAYING me for words since the mid 1990s, but it was in 2016 that my fiction career kicked off with *Myths & Magic*, my tribute to Terry Pratchett. I've written over 50 published novels since then, the vast majority of which, like this one, are post apocalyptic sci-fi. My stories focus on the power of the human spirit to triumph over seemingly impossible odds.

I live in the south of England with my wonderful wife.

Here's where you can find more from me...

Website: www.kevpartner.co.uk

My book library: books2read.com/rl/kevpartner

Follow me on Bookbub: bookbub.com/authors/kevin-partner

Facebook: www.fb.com/KevPartnerAuthor

Made in United States
North Haven, CT
11 February 2026

88540948R00136